THE DANCE

BY DAVE BRICKER

THE DANCE

By Dave Bricker
All Rights Reserved.
Copyright ©2009 Essential Absurdities Press

Cover and book design by David Bricker.

ISBN: 978-0-9843009-0-7

ESSENTIAL ABSURDITIES PRESS

http://www.theDanceNovel.com
http://www.essentialAbsurdities.com

...

For Ari

Chop wood, carry water.
After enlightenment, chop wood, carry water

-Zen Proverb

–Germany - April, 1970–

Hanns stepped from his apartment into the chill of a new morning. The last stars faded, leaving Venus hanging alone in a blackberry sky courting a waning sliver of moon over a thin streak of bubble gum. A loon called from the dark band of forest beyond the field ahead and his boots crunched lightly over remnants of the evening's frost on the grass. He moved briskly to warm himself yet did not particularly hurry. A rabbit crossed the road ahead. Hanns turned down the footpath and towards the forest.

Handsome with a strong jaw, shoulder-length blonde hair and an athletic build, Hanns was about thirty years old—clever, cynically witty, and filled with a sense of boyish wonder often catalyzed by tiny details of nature or design that eluded other people. He was apt to marvel at the veins of a leaf, could focus for hours turning small parts on a machinist's lathe, and would comfortably wait a small eternity for lighting and fortuitous circumstances to collaborate on setting up a perfect photograph. A student of the World, he read voraciously, and had a twinkle in his eye that had liberated many a young lady from her panties.

A still-purple scar above his knee stabbed slightly. Hanns winced but did not break his stride. A pleasant glow of exertion soon overcame both the chill and the pain in his thigh like a glass of warm brandy. The morning warmed and a crazed squiggle of orange sun appeared under the bubble gum that was now stuck to the lavender blanket of sky.

Having each awakened, Hanns and the landscape slowed their paces and breathed deeply. Following the path into the forest along a small stream, he looked up into the canopy of pine branches above and enjoyed the sunbeams and shadows fornicating playfully in the branches. This was his favorite time of the day. He always timed his morning walk so he could be present in the woods to witness the dawn's symphony of light and color.

Following the trail towards an old stone bridge that spanned the stream, Hanns grabbed at the camera that nearly always hung about his neck. The light was perfect and the reflections in the water were enchanting— but he let the shot go. Some moments can be captured and others refuse to be canned. Fumbling with a light meter, adjusting a camera and composing a frame are not always consistent with being wholly present in the moment. "I am not an observer this morning," thought Hanns. *"I am in it!"*

The Palatinate forest was an ancient and beautiful place where one would not be surprised to find a fairy ring in a secret clearing or stumble over an elf hiding his gold—a land of cuckoo clocks, fairy tales and ages-old magic. This was Hanns's childhood playground and he was at home here. As a boy, he had discovered mysterious places in these woods with stone cairns and carved runic figures, and had played in the ruins of medieval castles.

He mounted the footbridge and drew a pear from his pocket, taking a bite of the yellow fruit and chewing it slowly—savoring the tartness and texture, the cool, smooth flesh and how it melted on his tongue— a banquet in miniature for someone willing to stop and consume details, Hanns studied how the pear's red blush faded to golden green, taking it in as a local vintner might a fine Riesling.

An engineer by both education and inclination, Hanns found his attention drifting to the arrangement of stones on the bridge. He imagined ancient artisans pulling these stones from the stream bed, shaping them precisely with hand-tools and techniques lost to time, and arranging them functionally and attractively like some great puzzle into a span that would survive the elements for centuries. His musings were pregnant with a sense of *déjà vu*, partially because the patterns in these stones always triggered his curiosity, and partially because of his ancestral connection to this place. He sensed the lost secrets to making stone bridges were buried in his DNA—paved over by the modern world like a lovers' kiss in Pompeii—but still lurking just beneath the surface of his soul.

As with every visit to this bridge, he resolved to do some research on bridge-building. Surely, this material could be found in a library and Hanns expected a moment of realization just a page or two into his reading where the ancient, internal knowledge would break through—but such resolutions always stayed on the bridge with the spirits of those who built it. Hanns continued down the path where thoughts of stone masonry and ancient engineering were quickly eclipsed by the greenery, a chorus of birds, rustlings in the branches, and the soft sound of his boots on the earth.

Many years later on his death bed, Hanns would spontaneously recall his lifelong wish to understand the construction of the ancient bridge, and would ask a friend to bring a book on the subject. He was to expire only moments before the friend returned with a book containing impossibly unlikely diagrams of the very stone bridge upon which he now stood.

But it was *good* to be back here in these German woods. His escape from the Saudi desert only a few months before felt as if it had happened a lifetime ago. He had returned with a commercial pilot's license (compromised as it was by the threat of latent malaria), quite a few reels of film footage, a collection of photographs, a gash from a mortar shell fragment in his thigh, some money in his pocket and a certain sense of invincibility. Hanns was not a religious man, but recognized he was still alive only by virtue of a run of extraordinary good luck and a string of nearly impossible coincidences. But even in combination with the awareness of what good fortune it was to enjoy a jaunt in the woods on an April morning, this realization was not enough to send him plodding off to Church on Sundays (though he smiled when he considered what reactions a priest might have to his confessions).

The law of averages had clearly been suspended on his behalf, and he had certainly been the recipient of blessings in some form. It was impossible not to connect with *something* in this beautiful place, but like not taking a photograph at the wrong time, Hanns was content to simply be in the experience of that connection without attaching labels or rule books.

There are subtle signs that herald changes in weather or season that presage the more obvious ones. Such signs are invisible to most people though sailors and fugitives, mountain climbers, outlaws and gamblers all live and die by their abilities to read them. "This is all very pleasant…," thought Hanns as his path meandered through the forest, "but it's starting to feel awfully *easy*." The odd restlessness settled on his shoulders again and he smiled—not allowing the feeling to disturb him or ruin his walk . "Whatever is *next* is on its way."

The trail emerged from the woods and made a right angle turn along a fenced field. Neat wooden fence posts rode up and down gently with the landscape and Hanns rode these waves along the forest's edge. He closed one eye and played with the lines of perspective, observing how the angle of the tree line neatly complemented the angle of the fence line as the two triangles converged on the roofs of the village and the terminus of the path ahead. He did not shoot the photograph.

The path carried Hanns towards the village—a traditional German half-timbered affair that save for a half-hour's walk through the woods between them might just as well be the one he lived in. It still looked much as it had in the 1500's except for the additions of electrical wiring, street lights and modern vehicles.

Sensitive to the metaphorical context of his surroundings, Hanns found meaning in moving along a path, especially an earthen one. Though not part of a main road, the trail was wider here and rutted by the tires of tractors and small agricultural equipment as much by centuries of foot traffic. The grassy center between the tire tracks was dotted with tiny, yellow wildflowers. "A pretty road upon which to travel symbolically towards one's destiny," he mused.

At the bottom of a small hill at the town's entrance, an open, wooden gate invited travelers into a park containing a grove of shade trees. Within its bounds were several benches, a rather elaborate arrangement of wooden swings and ladders for children to play on—probably crafted by the townspeople, a pond upon which a few ducks paddled lazily, some pretty but not particularly artfully-executed arrangements of roses, and a wooden stage used for small concerts, amateur plays and occasional speeches at small celebrations— a pleasant if unremarkable place.

Upon the stage this morning sat an artist studying his canvas with intensity. He sported a great head of dark curly hair, a coarse mustache, a loose-fitting and unbuttoned shirt of white cotton bespattered with dabs of color, tight-fitting jeans with bell-bottoms, and a gold chain with a coin that dangled precariously close to the wet canvas as he leaned towards his easel. The morning had warmed considerably and as Hanns drew closer, he saw a glint of perspiration on the artist's brow, though it was impossible to tell whether this was due to the rising temperature or the man's intensity of focus. Tanned and dark like a Corsican pirate, the painter had a curious presence that Hanns felt immediately and from quite a distance.

The day was still young and the shadows long. Hanns approached quietly, smiling a silent and subtle greeting and with one finger, gestured first towards his camera and then towards the artist who acknowledged the request with only the subtlest raise of his eyebrows and the most minimal of nods. Hanns's intent had been to make his request of the painter discretely, almost invisibly so as not to disturb his focused state, and it was perhaps this same sensitivity that motivated the man to acquiesce instead of scowling him off. The artist continued to stare intently at his work, his brush poised as if waiting for a signal to stab the canvas. Hanns put his jacket aside and began to study his subject. For a while, he took no photos—just moved around slowly, experimenting with angles and observing how the sunlight created a glow around his subject's dark curls when the backlighting was just right. Hanns circled again with a light meter and jotted a few notes on a small pad kept in his shirt pocket. He was experienced enough as a photographer so that none of this was really necessary (and the notes were merely scribbles), but it was part of an acclimatization dance designed to ensure his camera was accepted rather than just tolerated in his subject's space. Whether any of this was conscious to the man with the paintbrush was impossible to tell, but after a few minutes, Hanns sensed his presence was no longer an intrusion, that his camera was not a distraction and that he had established himself, by virtue of his handling of his equipment and his respect for the space as a fellow artist who should be left equally undistracted to practice his art.

For the next half-hour, Hanns worked around the

painter, shooting images at every conceivable angle and often at uncomfortably close range. He even lay on the ground shooting up at the man's face with the sun behind his subject. Three rolls of film later, he was sweaty, covered with grass and dirt and yet, had captured his moment without disturbing the artist. The man continued dabbing at the canvas, occasionally arcing the brush dramatically—almost violently across his composition and then returning to a position of poise as if waiting for the canvas to present the next signal—all the while appearing oblivious to Hanns and his lens.

Hanns sipped gently from a bottle filled with tea. He thought of offering it to the artist who had developed dark circles of perspiration under his arms, but observed the man was still channeling his inspiration and thought better of it. The bottle was reinterred into the pocket of the jacket, which Hanns draped over a bench in the shade before sitting down on the ground in front of it cross-legged with his back against the lower seat. He closed his eyes and recounted the photos he had just shot in his mind's eye.

As if on cue, the legs of the easel upon which the painting sat now slowly began to spread outwards. The painting got lower and lower but at first, the artist didn't seem to notice. He crouched lower, working with the canvas as it made its slow descent. The legs of the easel were connected by small chains which prevented them from splaying completely but at the moment the chains became snug, the upper part of the assembly gave way and the painting dropped to the level of the man's knees.

"Mierda! Shit! Scheisse! Merde!" The painter looked surprised as if having suddenly awakened in front of his collapsed easel, realized the whole thing had happened without his noticing and that he must have looked absurd to the stranger with a camera who now sat a short distance away with a boyish grin on his face. The two began to laugh, lightly at first and then more heartily, each one provoking the other into a deeper celebration of life's fundamental absurdities. "Tino," offered the painter, extending a hand smeared with undried paint and sweat along with a smile that immediately suggested it belonged to a character capable of upholding the same high standards of hedonistic mischief as the person to whom it was extended. Hanns introduced himself and accepted the gesture warmly.

"Let me look at that easel," suggested Hanns. "Maybe I can fix it?"

He removed the painting gently and respectfully,

placing it out of the way, and began to look at the easel's adjustment apparatus. After a few moments, he pulled a pocket knife from a leather holster on his belt, opened a screwdriver blade and starting at the top, adjusted all the screws so they were not only tight, but had their slots turned in alignment with whatever wooden struts each was set into. For him, such repairs and adjustments were simple, and with the easel restored to working order, he suggested to Tino that he now need only check the screws periodically for any change in their rotation.

Quietly to himself, Hanns deferred to his "Christmas Lights" theory. Most strings of lights illuminate dutifully and consistently, humbly fulfilling their purpose. Others have bulbs that blink, flash intermittently, don't work at all or burn particularly brightly. It seemed that those with the most brilliant bulbs were typically the same ones that contained a few duds and blinkers. Hanns had known many artists; passionate and talented people who created works of inspired genius yet might not be able to use a screwdriver, make toast or read a map. He doubted Tino would keep track of the orientations of his easel's screw-slots (or that he would be comfortable tightening them himself anyway), but intuitively thought the bright or interestingly colored lights on this particular string worth getting to know. Certainly, a few dim bulbs were a small price to pay for creative company.

Hanns opened the easel back up, adjusted it to an elevation that looked more ergonomically functional than it had been when first set up, and placed Tino's canvas back on the cross-piece. He studied the work for a few moments—an abstract, cubist painting of a nude—rendered in oils with bold, passionate strokes and colors.

"Will you be here tomorrow?" asked Hanns. "I can make prints tonight and would be happy to bring you copies."

"If the weather is good, I'll be here," Tino replied. "I'll finish this piece tomorrow. When I'm done, I'd love to take you for breakfast with my wife."

The two shook hands again. Hanns slung his jacket over his shoulder. Tino thanked him again for taking the photographs and fixing the easel. Hanns brushed himself off one more time before continuing on his way towards the village.

Though he sensed a spark of connection with Tino, he was hesitant to meet the artist's wife. Hanns was well aware of his own strengths and weaknesses and he'd had more than one narrow escape involving the evasion of some passionate husband's detection. In these small villages where everyone was separated by very few degrees, he had developed a reputation among the young ladies in the short time since his return. Some nocturnal frolicking was always fun, but he had had his fill of conflict and trauma in the Middle East. This was a time to keep things simple and uncomplicated —qualities he imagined to be lacking in the wives of intense, passionate painters.

Tino's artwork was another matter. The style was really quite visionary, and definitely more artful than erotic, but Hanns could not help but to have noticed the disproportionately large vagina in Tino's painted figure—given his own interest in such things.

Leaving Tino and his easel behind, Hanns picked up his step, passed rows of white and brown gingerbread buildings with colorful shutters thrown wide to let in the morning light, arriving at what would be considered no more than a wide street in a larger town but what served as a plaza for this small village. The streets and sidewalks had evolved from the rutted path to a neat arrangement of cobblestones that Hanns never tired of staring at. The stones were arranged traditionally so that in spite of their uniformity, their patterns and groupings always seemed to shift and change—sometimes appearing as layers of ever-widening arcs and at other times forming fishscale groupings that appeared incongruous with the hard angles of rectangular streets and sidewalks. The street itself was barely wide enough for two cars to pass, having most likely been designed centuries before to accommodate horse traffic, though the sidewalks were wide around the plaza. A few small tables with umbrellas had been set out in front of small coffee shops and bakeries. The ground-floors of the buildings presented store fronts with bright awnings, painted signs and modern display windows. Upper floors contained mostly residences. Morning sounds of children, hair-dryers, televisions and pets wafted gently through windows as the occupants embraced the day. The villagers were mostly on the move by now—going off to jobs, seeking a cup of *espresso* to start the day with or perhaps making their way to the grocery store to poke the fruit and squeeze the bread.

Hanns loved this human zoo, never feeling quite like he really belonged to it, but that it was fascinating to observe. It all seemed simplistic to him—this routine of coming and going, working, eating, sleeping, fucking, having children, pissing, shitting, earning money, spending money, getting sick, dying—a not-altogether-unpleasant form of treading water. Sometimes he almost envied an ability he perceived in many people to embrace some chosen or prescribed illusory pattern of the orderly cobblestones of life. A lust for something different always nibbled at him—a new place, a new lover, another subject to film, a project, an invention— a new way to see beauty in the patterns of the stones. He half-wondered if all of his tiny revolutions might be more of a bother than a force of liberation to those who no longer perceived or enjoyed the dancing patterns just beneath their feet.

Buddhists equated desire with suffering but Hanns disagreed. Desire was just a prelude—titillating foreplay to pleasurable indulgence in a world full of wonder and plenty.

He entered a small café, and ordered a strawberry milkshake and a nut bread from a skinny young girl behind the counter who looked to have recently graduated from high school. Amused at being asked to make a milkshake at this hour of the morning, she couldn't suppress a smile.

"You have wonderful eyes," smiled Hanns. "You have made my morning."

The girl blushed, looked down and muttered, "thank you."

"Could you, my dear, find for me a large strawberry to perch upon my milkshake—preferably one that you, in your expert opinion, judge to be as sweet as your own smile?"

The girl turned around and after a brief flurry of ice cream scooping, blender whirring and rummaging in the freezer, returned with a tall shake studded with an almost comically large cluster of bright red strawberries, presenting it dramatically upon the counter with a playful curtsey.

Hanns glanced at the girl's name tag. "Thank you,

Greta, for your kindness and good cheer. I shall be patronizing your fine establishment again in short order and bid you the most pleasant of mornings."

He dropped a bill on the counter, took her finger tips in hand, kissed them cavalierly, grabbed his shocking pink glass with the crimson mound of berries on top, and spinning on his heels, headed out the door where he sat down at a dark green table under a large yellow and black umbrella.

Really, he had no particular interest in the girl. She was very young, not altogether attractive to him, and probably could have been manipulated far too easily into an emotionally vulnerable place, but Hanns enjoyed making her feel good and how little effort was required to do so. A mound of in-season, sweet strawberries seemed wonderful compensation for a bit of amusing flirtation.

Hanns leaned back in his chair and sipped his milkshake, his tall glass glowing like a shining beacon of pink rebellion against the green table and subdued surroundings. The nut bread was fresh—still warm—and full of raisins, dried apricots, and cinnamon. The soft crunch of sunflower seeds harmonized with the chewiness of rolled oats and a few unidentifiables.

After a few minutes, Greta came outside. "Would

you like some coffee, Mr.…uh…?"

"Hanns, my Dear. Please call me Hanns… but no thank you on the coffee. I'm quite happy with my strawberries."

The girl smiled and went back inside.

Hanns never understood why the world went crazy for caffeine when so much inspiration to jump up in the mornings naturally presented itself. He supposed many people sadly just weren't that excited about starting a new day. Moreover, coffee, and also beer seemed somewhat proletarian to him—not that he thought of himself as belonging to any sort of elite group—but with things like psilocybic mushrooms available for plucking in the local cow pasture, friends willing to offer an occasional bowl of good hashish and even the comparative complexity of a glass of fine wine, the quick buzzes, pick-me-ups and pharmaceutical crutches embraced by mainstream society as standard measures for navigating the days and weekends seemed uninspiring. Exploring the deep recesses of inner space had its times of appropriateness, but just being in the world presented plenty to get high upon. Though an occasional chemical gourmet, Hanns was not about to miss any of the good life because he was sped up, slowed down or turned around by something as mundane as caffeine or alcohol. Like any gourmet, he relied upon menu selection, portion control and good company to make the difference between a meal and an experience. For times like this morning, cobblestones, an innocent smile and strawberries were more than enough.

He sat quietly at his table, chewing on a pink-frosted berry. Briefly shooting dagger-eyes at a young man lighting a cigarette at the next table, he indicated with a cough and a sneer that such malodorous pollution of his space was an unacceptable affront. The smoker offered little real consideration to the idea that blowing smelly, toxic smoke next to someone's food could be offensive, but Hanns had enormous presence and didn't look worth confronting. Taking his coffee cup in hand, the man ground his cigarette butt under his shoe and left, averting his gaze to suggest that his decision to leave had nothing to do with Hanns.

Hanns politely picked up the butt and deposited it in the trash as much to purify the space as to make a statement about public smoking to anyone who might be watching, and then quickly banished the smoker from his mind.

Returning to his post as observer of life, he closed his eyes briefly, cleared his mind and thought clearly, as if to provoke some manifestation of his mental exercise in his physical world, "I am ready for whatever will happen *next*." He wished for nothing in particular. The meditation was simply an extension of what he had felt while walking on the path into the village; an acknowledgement to himself and a proclamation to whatever forces he might influence or be influenced by that he was *ready*.

Two women emerged from a shop on the other side of the plaza, talking as they strode over to the café. Looking about briefly at their seating options, they quickly settled on the table adjacent to Hanns and his pink strawberry milkshake which still radiated absurdity and rebellion in spite of its depleted state. The taller woman listened with controlled concern while the younger one, a slightly overweight girl of about twenty grew more and more frantic.

"I know…I'm sorry…I wish there was more time, but what can I do? Put off the wedding? Can we buy a machine? Borrow one? Rent one? What will I do with a half-finished gown?"

The woman listening was in her late-twenties— thin, wearing a long skirt printed with an intriguing geometric pattern, a yellow blouse that revealed just a tease of cleavage and brown hair tied back in a pony tail. She listened intently over round, frameless glasses, breathed deeply and closed her eyes.

"I have three machines—good ones—not your grandmother's sewing machines" she explained, "but one died yesterday afternoon. The other was fine last night but wouldn't work when we came in this morning. I have begged and pleaded but I can't get a service man out here for three days. I would use the third machine, but yours is not the only wedding happening this weekend, and my girls back in the shop are already fighting each other to use the one that's left."

The desperate bride began to tear up and sniffle. "Anna, isn't there something you can do?"

"I have no solid reassurances for you," she replied, "but I'll figure something out. I always do, but I have no idea yet what that will be. Rather than beat our heads on the table about it, let's have a bite and a drink. We'll get our heads together and see what comes our way."

Anna got up and headed into the café, leaving the bride-to-be sitting at the table feeling helpless and bewildered.

Hanns liked Anna's attitude. She was sharp, intelligent and professional, but not cold. She didn't ply her client with phony excuses and patronizing promises. He met few people who could naturally summon up that kind of blind faith in dumb luck, and Anna had an entirely unpretentious air about her that he found attractive. He always admired a pretty girl, but was easily bored by women who were vain, showy or even too quick to jump out of their clothes and into his bed. Not that he didn't find such women amusing, but those with a few more layers to peel were more challenging and more interesting.

Anna emerged from the cafe with two strawberry milkshakes in hand and a basket of nut rolls tucked under her arm. She looked at Hanns and raised an eyebrow. "Not my usual fare," she explained, "but for some reason you inspired me this morning."

The exchange and the ridiculousness of the three pink glasses provoked a weak smile from the teary bride.

"You are using Pfaff machines?" Hanns inquired.

Anna nodded.

"What models?"

"A 260 and a 360."

"Very nice," acknowledged Hanns smoothly.

"They worked flawlessly for the first few years, but lately have been giving me more and more trouble."

"I overheard you talking about them. Do you mind if I guess what's wrong with them?"

Anna and Hanns continued in the most matter-of-fact tones, neither of them consciously aware of the enormity of the coincidence—or perhaps both were entirely aware of it and had come to think of enormous coincidence as a matter of routine. Clearly, Anna fully expected to walk out on the street and have a sewing machine repairman fall in her lap. Hanns was already thinking about a number of things that might be entertaining to do in Anna's lap, but being called in to participate in the Universe's response to her predicament was a gentle reaffirmation of the magic of *whatever the hell it was*. Certainly, he was going to follow this road to whatever happened next.

"The one that worked last night can now no longer be adjusted. The lever is stuck at the top or bottom setting and it only works at the particular setting that you don't need at the moment, correct?"

Anna smiled affirmatively.

The young bride had incredulousness tattooed on her face, and placed her hand over a crucifix hanging at her neck. Hanns hoped Jesus really was alive in spirit as it would be a shame for him to have sacrificed so much only to miss out on all the boobies he got to hang between.

"This is a wilder guess...but has the second machine just been slowing down to a point where it is too sluggish to use—maybe over a week or so?"

"That's the one I originally placed a service call for," said Anna. "I was hoping to get it back up-to-speed before it died altogether. Unfortunately, I own a small shop and the service center is two hours away. There are much larger operations, closer to them, with more machines and big service contracts, which means the price I pay for first-rate equipment is second rate customer status…though that's starting to look like it may be less of a problem today."

"Anna," offered the dressmaker with a smile, extending a downturned hand.

"I am Hanns…." He accepted her fingertips firmly between his, "…and if you'll allow me, I shall do my best to respond to your pink beacons of distress." Hanns gestured at the strawberry shakes, thinking it best that any perceived double *entendre* might best be thought to have originated with his listeners.

The young bride had partially succumbed to hysteria. "Wait a minute! You're a sewing machine repair man? We came out here and just happened to sit down next to a sewing machine repairman? Anna, you don't find this to be at least a little bit unusual?"

"…But I'm not a sewing machine repairman," protested Hanns. "Sewing machine repair is way too boring. I am a pilot, sailor, photographer, film-maker, adventurer, engineer, designer, carpenter, mechanic, poet, prankster, slayer of damsels, romancer of dragons and psychedelic explorer. I only *dabble* with sewing machines and then, only under the most dire of circumstances."

Anna smiled and suppressed a giggle, shooting a glance at Hanns. She was sitting with a client and wasn't quite sure how overtly she should encourage Hanns's playful irreverence during a business meeting —however informal. Certainly, though, the day was getting more interesting and life's bumps always go down better with a comic chaser.

"Long story," explained Hanns. "Old girlfriend, a boat full of old sails and a long way home… not really worth telling…but I do have some experience keeping a sewing machine running and a faded souvenir ticket stub from a very long bus ride. Finish your milkshakes and I'll see if I can't get you back in action." Hanns deadpanned this last suggestion with control that would have been invisible to anyone less perceptive than Anna who herself masked any sign of response to it with the same measure of aplomb.

The astonished bride had already vacuumed her shake to the bottom and was now noisily and unself-consciously siphoning the last puddles of pink from the bottom of her glass with a white paper straw. Anna left her shake half-finished and nibbled on the strawberry she had saved for a grand finale.

"Hanns and I will go see to the machines," offered Anna to her client. "Take the nut rolls, Lisa, and I'll call in an hour or so with a status report."

"Thank you so much," offered the bride to Hanns, her eyes pleading with desperation, gratitude and lingering disbelief.

Hanns smiled, reached up and tipped an imaginary hat to the young woman who trotted off around the corner to be frantic about some other aspect of her wedding preparations.

Anna and Hanns each wiped off their tables, placed dirty saucers and glasses in the empty bread-baskets as a courtesy, and headed off across the street to a small shop door under a burgundy awning where an artfully painted sign on the window proclaimed:

ANNA

Flowers • Chocolate • Formal Wear • Intimate Apparel

Magical Accessories for the Dance

The green door swung open with a jingling of bells, wind chimes and other percussive paraphernalia hung on its interior to cheerfully announce the entrance or egress of patrons to Anna's shop. The room seemed somehow larger inside than on the outside, and had a definitively feminine presence about it such that many men would have felt as if they had walked into the women's lavatory. Terraced shelves on either side of the door offered potted flowers, including a selection of tropical orchids. Such flora were certainly not native to the Palatinate, and Hanns paused to inspect them. Some had comic faces, others looked like butterflies on a vine. Each had a unique perfume, some smelling like vanilla and others like—*what was that?*

Anna was pleased to have someone appreciate her collection as something warranting a description more respectable than "pretty flowers" or "unusual plants."

"Traditional floral arrangements are fine for funerals," she explained, "but I've never understood people's obsessions with killing things. Cut flowers are beautiful for a few days and then they wither and wilt—

terrible symbolism, especially for a marriage, don't you think?"

Hanns smiled his understanding.

"Orchids, with a little care, can last for decades—blooming over and over—returning again and again with exotic colors, ethereal scents and a reminder that nature and beauty are cyclical and changing. Yes, there's more maintenance involved, but the rewards are far sweeter, and as a metaphor you'd want anywhere near a marriage, it's far more powerful than the bittersweet old roses and thorns thing that was probably contrived as a marketing ploy to sell the prickly little weeds in the first place.'

'Beyond this, one of the great, largely unspoken quasi-secrets of humanity is that flowers are erotic—nature's vaginas on a stem. I think everyone knows this obvious truth on some level, but perhaps we prefer to keep the connection confined to less-conscious psychological and spiritual realms? Society has not evolved to a point where most women could appreciate being given a bunch of vaginas. Women have all been trained to respond to that kind of thing with a slap in the face, and most men can't handle being given flowers at all—even if I can't think of a more potent invitation to jump into bed.'

'The flower is literally the plant's reproductive organ. The similarity of many of them to the human article is sufficient to suggest the involvement of some form of higher mischief.'

'I'm delighted to see I'm not boring you…"

"With all this talk of vaginas?" interrupted Hanns with a grin. "Don't look at me. I never touch the stuff."

Anna laughed and moved over to a display case full of assorted chocolates.

"Endorphins," remarked Hanns.

"Precisely," continued his host, "but the real secret is olfaction—not molding them into droll little hearts and cupids. Catch the smell of brownies cooking or get a whiff of hot chocolate—that's what gets people tripping. You may notice my selection is rather limited as far as visual configuration goes, but try this…" She handed Hanns a tiny burgundy-colored canister with a gold-foil "ANNA" logo on the lid.

Upon popping it open with a thumbnail, a tiny hiss was heard and a breath of warm, dark, chocolate surrounded him. A single mouthful melted instantly on his tongue, clinging delicately and lingering inside his mouth while he inhaled slowly and deeply.

"You've heard of Hershey's kisses?" Anna asked rhetorically. "In select company, I call these 'Anna's

Orgasms'—though I haven't honestly wanted to put up with the kind of fallout I'd get from marketing them as such in a provincial place like this. If you like them, I'll let you try some of the really far-out ones; chocolate with balsamic vinegar, pepper, cumin, even garlic and a few I'd rather enjoy watching you guess at.'

'And on that note, sir, it's been a great pleasure introducing you to my little fiefdom, but I'm wondering if I might now persuade you to have a look at a few sewing machines I would dearly love to have coaxed back into some semblance of functionality."

Hanns was disappointed that Anna's tour had stopped short of "intimate apparel," but she probably expected him to request it, and he thought better of being predictable. He did like that someone made it her business to dispense erotic magic, and he respected the comfort with which Anna spoke about her art. However, her talk, chocolate, cavalier attitude and unglamorously natural good looks already had him fighting an erection and he thought it best to stay in alliance with rational forces. Clearly, a much larger plot was forming here than "boink the dressmaker" and with a sense that whatever was *next* had now started to happen, he thanked her for the chocolate and followed her past a counter into the back room. Anna had not asked him up-front for terms of payment, and he accepted the extension of her trust and vulnerability as a friendly gesture.

"What tools do you have handy?"

Anna went to a workbench and pulled from beneath it a metal box containing a collection of miscellaneous screwdrivers, wrenches, hammers and other odds and ends that had been slowly accumulated piecemeal over the years as things needed fixing. She presented this to Hanns along with a shoebox containing various sewing machine parts and accessories, some of which were old, some of which were broken and some of which had been forgotten before ever being used.

"And oil? Do you have good sewing machine oil? Very important."

Anna rummaged around in a cabinet and returned with a small brass oil can, tarnished and covered with a spattered patina of dried lubricant.

In a few minutes, Hanns had the lever heads, knobs, dials and faceplates off the machine with the stuck setting lever.

"These machines have a linkage with an elbow in it," Hanns explained. "The elbow has a pin that is under a certain amount of tension. Over time, the elbow pin wears in the hole and the linkage gets more and more wobble in it until finally, one day, you slide the lever to the top or bottom position and the elbow locks up. Can you see how the hole is worn into an oval shape?" He held up the linkage arm.

Anna nodded.

"I'll come back tomorrow with a bushing for the hole—we'll drill it, fill it, and just put a new hole into the old one, but that won't help you today. As this is a dress shop, I imagine you have a coat hanger around?"

Anna walked out and returned with a wire hanger.

"Perfect. Since you need this machine to work today, I'm going to use the hanger wire to create some guides that will keep the linkage from moving too far to one side or the other. I don't recommend you move the lever around any more than you have to— especially to the extreme ends of the setting range— but this will get you running again."

Within a few minutes, Hanns, with a pair of pliers, a wire cutter and a nail-file, had fabricated four pieces of coat-hanger into tiny linkage guides that looked as if they were part of the machine's original manufacture. The ends were curved precisely to the shape of the linkage arm on one side and had been bent on the other to the shape of a steel beam in the machine's chassis. Each popped into place with a satisfying snap.

Inspecting the rest of the mechanism, he added the

tiniest drops of oil before reassembling the machine, smiling as he smoothly slid the setting lever up and down.

Anna and her seamstresses had been watching intently, and now, a half-hour later, the first machine was fixed.

"What's all this standing around?" asked Hanns in mock business tone. "Doesn't anyone work for their money around here?" The seamstresses giggled and one of the girls grabbed up a big pile of shiny, white fabric that Hanns supposed would now become a wedding gown after all.

After fumbling around inside the second machine for a few minutes and disassembling a few components, Hanns raised his hand triumphantly in front of the sewing table's work light, a curly piece of greasy black thread hanging from his fingertips. "I pulled this from around the drive shaft…a common problem. Can you bring me some toothpaste and a rag?"

"Toothpaste?" Anna saw he was serious and returned a moment later with the requested items.

Hanns started the machine, stepped on the pedal and applied toothpaste with the rag to the shaft which soon shone like a mirror.

"Normally, I would use jeweler's rouge or rubbing

compound, but toothpaste contains microscopic pieces of pumice that make an excellent polishing medium… and it tastes good, too.'

'Now, let me show you something…."

Hanns grabbed the oil can. "Many problems are actually caused by too much oil. Do you see all the dried oil on the oil can? Touch it."

Anna and the remaining seamstress extended fingers.

"It's sticky…like pine sap," commented the seamstress.

"Exactly," smiled Hanns. "People often think 'more is better' when it comes to oil, but the excess just ends up catching dust and hardening into tar. Every few years, you should tear these things down and get rid of the old oil with a cleaning solution, but for general maintenance, it's important to resist the temptation to soak everything with lubricant."

He took a piece of the coat hanger wire, dipped it into the oil can spout and showed the girls how to put tiny drops of oil only where they were needed. Hanns reassembled the machine and flipped the switch. The motor hummed to life and he sewed a neat row of stitches across the toothpaste rag.

"I'm afraid I've outlived my usefulness here," sighed

Hanns, "and I was just starting to feel at home, cursed as I am with a dreaded Y-chromosome." Hanns wiped off the tools and placed them neatly back in their box, adding a drop of oil to the pliers as he did so.

Anna smiled. She had known something would happen to get the *Magical Accessories* shop dancing again. That was the just the magical way things worked, and she sensed it was no different for Hanns.

Hanns followed her wordlessly, past the busy seamstresses, dress-dummies, rolls of fabric, small dressing rooms and up the stairs through a door marked "PRIVATE."

At the top of the stairs, the door opened into a large room—a gallery of sorts. A low, oriental table sat in the center of the room surrounded by a rectangle of canvas cushions. Spacious oak floors extended to white walls that were mostly blank except for a small grouping of paintings and prints in simple black frames to one side. In a corner squatted a traffic light. The red, yellow and green lights labelled respectively, "DON'T FUCK", "IS IT LOVE?" and "FUCK." Sounds of flamenco guitar music drifted down from the floor above.

A window in the far wall revealed a busy kitchen entirely in contrast with the living and dining area. A large, stainless steel gas stove better suited to a restaurant kitchen than a residential one loomed beside a wide, steel counter top. Over the stove from beneath a great steel fume hood hung a whimsical collection of unmatched skillets and saucepans, the copper-bottomed ones patinaed green and brown from repeated use. Over the food preparation area, several small hammocks offered a colorful display of fresh fruits and vegetables.

"Make yourself comfortable and I'll start some lunch. What will you be drinking?"

"Water," replied Hanns, "a tall glass of water with no ice."

"A man after my own heart." Anna stepped into the kitchen through a saloon-style restaurant door with a window in the top and returned a moment later with a porcelain pitcher and a pair of glasses with cucumber slices perched on their rims—"Something different and refreshing."

Actually, it wasn't Anna's heart Hanns was after, but first impulses had begun to yield to curiosity. He was surprised to have been invited upstairs at this, their first meeting, and perhaps for the first time in his life, considered he might actually be in the company of someone who regarded *him* as sexual prey. This was clearly not a woman who would succumb to sweet talk or swoon over tales of adventure. She appeared interested in him (or she wouldn't have invited him upstairs), but the direction of that interest was yet to be expressed. Hanns laughed inwardly at himself. Here was someone who actually had *him* off balance. It would be interesting to see how this played out.

Anna returned to the kitchen. He watched her through the kitchen window as she deftly cut and combined ingredients in a small sauce pan. "You don't strike me as the meat and potatoes type," she observed.

"Are you okay with one of my vegetarian concoctions?"

Hanns was no vegetarian. He found the idea contrary to his working philosophy of "everything in moderation," (a philosophy he adhered to in moderation) but lately he had found himself naturally drifting more and more in a meatless direction. "If you're cooking it, I can only imagine it is somehow engineered through science or magic to stimulate the mind or erogenous zones in some delightful way. I look forward both to the taste and to hearing how you refer to this dish in familiar company."

Anna laughed and came back into the room.

"You are a most interesting man." She sat down on the cushion beside him. "I would like to know more about you."

"What can I tell you? I'm German-Swiss, spent most of my childhood here in the Palatinate, and trained as a mechanical engineer. I went to the Middle East as a pilot, got a commercial rating and flew until I came down with malaria and got grounded. As I recovered, I started doing documentary filmmaking work for the King. I was the only person there who could think in terms of perspective, depth of field, lighting and camera angle. They put me in charge, and I had a great time, kept the equipment working in that dusty environment, and developed a passion for serious filmmaking.'

'As things often do in that part of the World, it all blew up rather suddenly. I found myself unexpectedly filming a rather nasty military engagement in which my assistant was killed and I took a rather nasty chunk of mortar shell in my leg.'

'Then, they wanted to kill me…"

"Let me guess," interrupted Anna, "the King's daughter?"

"I'm glad you think so highly of me, but unfortunately, it was just people and petty politics. We were photographing documents for the government. A few went missing. I was set up to look like the foreign spy who might have an interest in such things, and was fortunate enough to escape through a series of impossibly timed doors and coincidences that would take me quite some time to regale you with. Needless to say, I am alive and well, here, and…"

Anna placed a fingertip on his lips. Withdrawing the finger and placing her hand on his, she pressed her lips lightly against his.

He pressed back.

She squeezed his hand.

He stroked her cheek with a finger.

She brushed his upper lip with the tip of her tongue.

He responded with his, gently circling her mouth as she opened it but not quite entering it.

Flamenco guitar music continued to drift down the stairs, mixing intoxicatingly with the aromas of Anna's spices in the kitchen, the smell of her hair and a hint of perfume—*what was that?* Anna and Hanns continued their dance for an agonizingly long time; baiting each other, teasing each other, circling each other but never quite losing balance.

Anna reached up, tweaked a single button and her blouse magically fell away, revealing a white bra with lace edges on the cups over which peeked the barest hints of the tops of her nipples.

In that instant, a number of thoughts occurred to Hanns, all simultaneously competing for priority attention. He wondered if this psychodrama was really happening or if it was all in his head, making the whole exercise in balancing and holding back rather pointless. He also wondered if his sense of imbalance was not happening by Anna's design—which would provide him with a much-desired excuse to ignore it altogether. Anna had just removed her blouse, so he suspected she was equally affected, but he couldn't be sure she wasn't just bringing in the heavy artillery. These fleeting thoughts were mostly overwhelmed by a great curiosity to see what those marvelous breasts looked like. If a contest of any kind was happening here, it would be neither unpleasant nor demoralizing to concede defeat at this point. He had stayed in the ring for a respectable time. If he didn't have a white flag handy, he certainly had a mast. Hanns resigned himself to a most glorious surrender.

The guitar music swelled, crescendoed and stopped. Hanns kissed Anna, gently pressed a finger to her chest and moved it slowly down between her breasts towards the little clasp.

"Whatever idiots engineered the hardware for bras were clearly homosexual men," thought Hanns. He hated these things, and fumbled with the mechanism, tugging, twisting, trying not to ruin the moment.

"Magical accessories for the dance," whispered Anna, pressing the center of the clasp with a finger. The cups fell away and Hanns forced himself to first look up into Anna's eyes—and then he saw past them.

Standing behind her at the bottom of the stairs was a rather large male figure. As his focus shifted from Anna's eyes to the stairs, the figure revealed itself to be none other than Tino, the artist he had met that same morning. He envisioned throwing himself through the second story window, into the awning below and onto the street, until he noticed the looks of amusement on Tino's and Anna's faces.

"Tino!" said Hanns in as casual a tone as he could muster. "I had no idea you come here, too!"

Tino laughed. "I see you were unable to wait until tomorrow to meet my lovely wife, but it looks like you're getting on quite well.'

'I'm sorry to interrupt you my dear, but I smelled something delightful in the kitchen and my nose conspired with my stomach to drag me downstairs. I believe I'll go back up to the studio and practice for another hour. I'll ask you to please not disturb me until lunch is ready." Tino's smile was as mischievously-spiced as any of Anna's exotic chocolates as he bounced back up the stairs.

The passionate sounds of flamenco guitar again drifted down and encircled them, ebbing and flowing like an ethereal tide of honeyed mist.

"I can get dressed if you've lost interest," teased Anna, concealing her breasts with crossed arms and feigning a look of embarrassed exposure.

"But…"

"Not only okay, but now officially sanctioned," giggled Anna, stepping out of the skirt that had just fallen about her ankles.

She kissed him tenderly and tugged at his belt buckle. "I hate these things," she said. "They'd be so much easier to take off if they'd been designed by homosexual men."

Anna and Hanns lay on the cushions, smiling and spent.

"Did you learn anything you wanted to know about me?"

"Sex," explained Anna, "if you'll indulge me in a long answer to a short question, is one of life's essential absurdities—something intrinsic to all of us—and inherently full of contradictions that each of us confronts in a different way.'

'Women are programmed for procreation and men are programmed for propagation. In other words, women make families. Men cause babies…and whether we acknowledge it or not, just beneath the surface, sex is fundamentally connected to baby-making. Women try to be attractive in order to procure a mate who can provide for them and their offspring. Men respond to the call of an attractive partner but not usually because they want a family to provide for. The motives are different, but each has something to offer the other and the dance begins.'

'…And we all know that rubbing the nerve endings is only part of the trip. Sights, smells, tastes and sounds combine with touch to make sex a gourmet banquet instead of a vending machine snack. Every sense must be stimulated and heightened to have a truly bed-breaking orgasm—and to fulfill nature's purpose of manufacturing more little absurdly contradicted people, we're hard-wired to be fascinated with sights, smells, tastes, sounds and sensations that must be delivered by a partner—which is part of where the absurdity comes in. It takes two to tango. Otherwise, we'd never complicate our lives by dancing with partners who have such a different agenda.'

'As children, we grow up naive, happy and free from sexual conflict until one day, girls start bleeding and realize all the boys are staring at their boobies, and boys start waking up with their pajamas full of semen. Most of the guidance offered by our society for understanding these changes consists of instructions to repress, abstain and focus on being "good." But because these urges and instincts are programmed into our DNA and cannot be genuinely overcome, many people feel weak or ashamed at their powerlessness to rise above them.'

'Add to this that sex has components of both dominance and surrender. We are no more in control when we have an orgasm than when we sneeze—

so to complicate matters, in order to have great sex, we require partners with whom we can be naked, scream, moan, quake and quiver; all helpless behaviors we wouldn't display out on the street. Women are fundamentally the receivers so unless there's a hostile takeover, men don't get any unless a woman gives it up. There's certainly surrender there, but let's not forget that men can be pushed over by a feather after a good climax. On some level, we all need a partner we can surrender to…'

'…which is contradictory to all the power and dominance aspects of the dance. When people with different agendas want something from one another, any number of different manipulations, deals, games, lies and subterfuges emerge to complicate the choreography. Women love strength and dominance in men, but also love having power over them with their sexual allure. Men want women to submit to their advances but are easily bored with fish that jump in the boat without a fight. Conquest is part of the ritual—part of the dance—and comes in forms ranging from gift-giving to playing hard-to-get.'

'But you can learn a tremendous amount from someone by dancing with them. Can they lead? Can they follow? Do they step on your feet? Do they have rhythm? Are they elegant? Sensitive?"

"So you wanted to see if I could *dance?*" interrupted Hanns with a note of skepticism.

"In *Tai Chi Chuan,*" Anna continued, "there is an exercise called "Pushing Hands" that retrains a person's natural instinct to resist force with force. Students are taught instead to yield naturally to force; to redirect it, responding with pressure only when their opponent is pulling back. I'm not a martial artist, but I see merit in both the practice and the metaphor. I call my version "pushing tongues." It's a little more exciting than "pushing hands," and it reveals a lot about people and their sexual orientation to power. You picked up on the game immediately, I noticed.'

'Everyone can dance, but few can dance *well.* You and I, if I can trust my reading, are both people who seek balance between dominance and surrender. We indulge in life's pleasures but are thinking, feeling people who receive life on many levels. Offered a kiss, many men would have simply jumped on me—and given that I find you attractive, that wouldn't have been such a terrible thing, but I thought we might establish a rhythm, some balance and, need I say, some mutual respect before we surrendered to our animal tendencies.'

'Some people's tastes never rise above swigging

cola, but a wine lover appreciates his grapes on many levels; opening the bottle, sniffing the cork, allowing the wine to breathe, swirling the drink in a delicate glass, and inhaling the bouquet before tasting the tiniest sip. The wine is sampled on different parts of the tongue that detect sweet, sour, salt and other flavors. A glass of soda on ice can be refreshing but is ultimately forgettable, unremarkable and pedestrian. I wanted to see what else we might serve here.'

'As a man, your tastes may run a broader spectrum and are likely driven by different biological forces, but at this stage of my life, I'm afraid I have become a helpless gourmet…and I must add that today's "wine" was most satisfying. I have a wonderful buzz on. Thank you."

Hanns nodded and tipped his imaginary hat again. "But you are a married woman…"

"With a six year old child who will soon be coming home from school so regrettably, we have to put our clothes back on…but let me answer your entirely reasonable questions."

Hanns and Anna arose and began sifting through the clothing strewn around the room. Anna continued as they reassembled themselves. "My husband and I love one another dearly. We are soul-mates, understanding one another deeply, naturally and completely. I assure you that sexually, he is more than capable, and we have a regular and rather creative sex life. Under normal circumstances, I think we could keep one another interested, entertained and exhausted, but life does not always offer normal circumstances."

Hanns raised an inquisitive eyebrow.

"Many women fantasize about finding a man who is 'hung like a horse.' I ended up with one who is hung like an elephant. Tino is blessed or cursed with a mutant penis. Psychologically and spiritually, we are absolutely meant for one another. Anatomically speaking, I'm not sure if the pain was greater conceiving our son or giving birth to him. Needless to say, we have evolved plenty of gymnastic approaches to sharing pleasure and affection, but deep down, we humans are pre-wired for copulation. Certain pleasures and certain states of mind can only be realized through the act of intercourse.'

'After some frustrating time together, we discovered that even in the best of friendships and marriages, one partner cannot be all things to the other. We trust one another, love one another and see ourselves as a happy couple. In fact, we're a happier couple since we began supplementing our sex life with external sources of fulfillment.'

'Tino is a young man, and at the risk of sounding

condescending, what he really needs is just a stream of pretty girls with big vaginas who want their giant penis fantasies fulfilled. He also happens to have an insatiable sexual appetite—which is where you come in."

Hanns threw Anna a curious glance.

Anna chuckled. "Nothing at all like that, I assure you. I'll keep you for my own evil purposes if I can, but you're clearly a man of experience. I know this from having just had some wonderful sex with you, and also from my position as owner of a dress shop which attracts gossiping girls from all over Germany. Your reputation precedes you, but if you have encountered…"

Hanns smiled. "I confess I've met a few women I dodge for that reason. It's like fuc…"

"Spare the masculine similes for Tino" smirked Anna, "but if you can help keep my husband supplied with capacious young women, you'd be doing us both a favor."

"Easily accomplished. Maybe we can double date and pull a switcheroo?" Hanns joked. "But what is *Anna* really looking for; clearly not an alternate marriage, but clearly more than soda on ice?"

"Initially, it was entertaining for me to play the seductress, charm the pants off a few high-school boy toys and have my pleasures, but that was awfully easy and most were more interested in completing the sex act than luxuriating in it. To be honest, most men don't get any better with age. As I told you, I'm a hopeless gourmet.'

'I'm also a woman, which means I'm not really wired for sexual predation. I don't need the same distinctions between meaningful and merely recreational relationships that many men require to rationalize staying focussed on who they're officially married to. That approach got boring for me. I found it empowering at first to seduce someone ten years younger than myself, but it's a false reflection. I'm not a trophy hunter at heart.'

'But as a woman, I'm a creature of intuition, and based on what I observed downstairs in my shop of your skills, talent, focus, wit and good looks, I thought you just might make an excellent pleasure buddy—someone who could engage in some gourmet love-making, but also in some gourmet conversation, appreciate an unusual meal and perhaps challenge me. I suppose I'm looking to supplement my marriage with something more worthwhile than "ring and run."'

'I also imagine you're something of a free spirit who would be just as happy to relegate the day-to-day politics of marriage to someone else, but in spite of that, I believe you're an *aficionado* of the dance—someone who leads, follows, mixes styles, swings, waltzes and boogies down—and the essential absurdities dictate that such things require practice, time and a dedicated partner."

Tino had come down the stairs and was now bringing a tray to the table upon which sat three white porcelain bowls with matching spoons, a stack of paper cocktail napkins and three glasses of wine. Grinning playfully at Hanns and Anna who were still clearly a bit red-faced, he placed the food on the table and pushed the bowls and glasses gently towards them. "*Bon apetit.*"

"Well," offered Hanns to Anna with mock seriousness and clearly feigned disinterest, "being that I'm only a man, you know not to take any declaration of commitment or ongoing interest I might make too seriously, but I do have some business in this area tomorrow installing a bushing in a sewing machine and dropping off some photographs. If you're inclined to work on a few dance steps, I'll try not to trip over your feet."

Anna laughed.

"And that was you playing the guitar upstairs?" Hanns asked, turning to Tino.

"One of my two great passions," Tino explained.

"Flamenco is for me the ultimate 'magical accessory for the dance.' In fact, it is a musical style developed specifically for accompanying *cante* and *baile*—singing and dancing. The *compás* is the heartbeat of flamenco— the *Bulerías, Cañas, Alegrías* and others are rhythmic styles of flamenco practiced by both the dancer and the *tocaor*—the player. The *Guitarrista* who cannot keep *compás* is shunned and will never be invited to play or perform, but those who can keep time and drive time, those who have the *toque,* inspire the dancers to passion.'

'When I saw you were about to indulge in the inestimable pleasure of *bailando* with my dear Anna, and when I recalled the passion with which you approached your photography this morning, I took it upon myself to contribute some of my own inspiration in the form of musical accompaniment. I trust it was to your liking?"

"Marvelous," returned Hanns, "as is this soup."

Anna smiled and nodded.

As they finished their meal, Tino recalled the events of earlier that morning to Anna and how Hanns had photographed him painting in the park and repaired his easel.

"My friends," said Hanns, wiping the corner of his mouth with a napkin. "I thank you for the hospitality, for your very broad definition of that word, for the music, conversation, wine and a delightful lunch. If you'll forgive me, I have some work to do in the darkroom and on my machinist's bench this afternoon, and this must all get done before some very important business I've committed to tomorrow morning."

"The pleasure is ours," replied Anna. "However, I do hope you'll not make a whore of me by refusing to invoice my shop for your repair work."

"On the contrary. I do hope you won't reduce my visit to a mere service call by refusing a gesture of friendship."

"*Touché*," laughed Anna. "If friendship is to be our medium of exchange, I'm more than comfortable with that currency. Thank you."

Hanns shook Tino's hand, kissed Anna on the cheek and made his way down the stairs, through the dress shop where the seamstresses proffered knowing smiles, past a now much calmer young bride-to-be trying on the beginnings of her wedding gown—which through Anna's magic, appeared to have caused her to shed quite a bit of weight—past the chocolates and orchids, across the plaza and down the street, through the park, down the path next to the fences and fields, into the woods, across the bridge (where he momentarily made a mental note to read up on bridge construction) and back across the field to his apartment.

"If this is *next*, I quite like it so far," mused Hanns to himself as he deftly loaded film into development canisters in the pitch black of his dark room. "It's been a most interesting day."

As promised, Hanns met Tino in the park the next morning with a large manila envelope under one arm and a silver attaché case in the other.

Tino was putting the finishing strokes on his painting. The easel held firm this time, and Hanns admired the work. Tino's passionate nature revealed itself through bold brushwork and a powerful refinement in color choices. Fine details faded into thick, impasto paint. A dancer graced the canvas, nude but for a pair of castanets held high above her head in one hand and a flurry of red handkerchief in the other—dynamic, vibrant and moving to the music of an abstract guitarist behind her who could easily have been dismissed as part of the swirling background by someone with a less discriminating eye, but who, with careful observation could be seen to have his head tossed back and his right hand flailing across the strings.

"I can see this isn't your first painting," joked Hanns. "That's quite a wonderful composition."

"Since I was a small boy, all I wanted to do was paint and play the guitar. The other kids teased me because I liked art and music over playing sports...until

I beat the crap out of them and they left me alone, but I have always known what I wanted to do. If my parents had not threatened to take away my paints and my guitar, I would never even have gone to school.'

'I am Basque—born in the crazy north of Spain. My mother was a gypsy, and my father's job kept us moving around Europe during the first part of my life. By the time I was twelve, I spoke five languages and around that time, we finally settled in the South of Spain. There I began to study the techniques and culture of flamenco.

'In University, they would not let me study both painting and guitar. They said it was impossible to do well in two disciplines so I chose painting. It was just as well, as the guitar department still looked upon flamenco as a form of folk music—not worthy of serious academic study. I painted by day, studying the Masters and trying to develop a style of my own. At night, I played in the flamenco clubs and chased the flamenco dancers—a magnificent time, though I remember far too little of it; I didn't sleep very much.'

'For my final project, I did an interpretation of da Vinci's *Last Supper*. In the center, where Jesus presides over the table, I copied da Vinci down to the tiniest brush stroke, but in the original image, Jesus and the disciples are sitting in a room with windows behind them and panels on the wall. I used these boxes as boundaries and within each, I interpreted the original painting in the hand of a different artist, even bringing in commercial styles, as if Monet, Van Gogh, Paul Klee, Kurt Schwitters, Herbert Bayer, Pablo Picasso, Andy Warhol, Reid Miles and a few advertising agencies had all contributed to the work. In the center, I added a touch of my own; on the table in front of Jesus's outstretched hands I painted a top hat and a small white rabbit.'

'The school was outraged—mostly over the top hat and the rabbit. Some of the faculty tried to prevent my graduation, but the work demonstrated that the requirements had been met, and the controversy brought admirers and critics to the graduation show from miles around. At the gallery opening, I just sat there in a corner, playing flamenco, listening, and let people wonder who the artist was. Some people were angry—crying—almost violent. It was the only time in my life I ever wore a big crucifix around my neck for protection."

Hanns laughed. "So you pretended to be the hired music stooge at your own gallery opening?"

Tino wrapped his canvas and put it under his arm,

slung his folded easel over his shoulder, and the two began walking together down the cobblestone road toward the village.

"It was amazing how quickly the doctrines of forgiveness, turn the other cheek, and seek the truth, were abandoned when these people's fragile belief systems were threatened—not even threatened really, but merely satirized—without any malice on my part. Other bastardizations of masterworks appeared in my show along with a few mischievous pieces of my own design. I still have a few of them in my studio I can show you. I had originally planned to reveal myself as the artist at the show, but a few people in the crowd that night made me think better of it.

'Hanns, I don't know if I believe in God or not. I think it's more ignorant to settle on a belief system than to remain open minded and inquisitive. People "make up their minds" like they make up their beds or their faces in the morning, but most are just avoiding the discomfort of not knowing; they are afraid of the very mysteries that excite me…the very mysteries that make life an adventurous voyage of discovery.

But if there is a God, He has a sense of humor. Especially, if it were true that an omnipotent being was powerful enough to create oceans, mountains, and life on earth, I cannot, in my wildest imagining, conceive that such a being would be such a *pussy* as to be offended by a mere painting. If you consider the way we humans behave, the platypus, the black widow spider who eats her mate, lemmings, whales that live in the deep ocean yet breath air or listen to Anna talk about sex, you can readily observe the world is full of absurdity. If these absurdities are God's creations, I think we should try to understand His divine jokes enough to laugh at them. If He's the original Old Master, we only stand to gain by studying his sense of humor and copying his style."

"As far as I'm concerned," said Hanns, "Religion is just something that brings people together so they can all agree to *not* know the same things as a group. We are both artists. We find truth, humor and beauty in the world and each in our own way, we preserve it, interpret it, channel it and share it. What could be more divine than pointing out the details of God's world? So many people dwell on where all this marvelous experience came *from*. I can't say I'm not interested, but it's origins are not nearly as important as what it *is*. Too many miraculous sunrises are obscured by stained glass windows. Too many people sit in dark, empty rooms thinking the lights will come on at the moment of their death. Whether by evolution or by design, we have a capacity to enjoy, to reflect, to think, to feel, to experience. Whether by evolution or by design, the world is full of beauty, tragedy, truth, deception, surprises, predictability, adventure, absurdity and beautiful women. Evolution or design? Who cares? We're here...*now*. Would you like to jump first?'

Hanns pantomimed opening a large sliding door and jumping from an airplane with arms and legs extended. Tino followed him in mock jump through the imaginary portal.

The two continued across the plaza, laughing and carrying their gear.

"Which reminds me...I have something for you, Tino."

Hanns handed Tino a folded piece of paper. I've listed a few...er...prospects for you in no particular order. Hanns glanced down at what looked like a tennis ball canister shoved inside Tino's pants. I've added a few notes for each on where to find them or what excuses to use for having their numbers. Let me know when you need more and do tell me how things work out."

Tino stopped and put his hand to his chest, staggered and looked to the sky like a desert traveler who had just seen an oasis over the horizon. In exaggerated relief, he embraced Hanns. "Thank you! Thank you for a place to quench my burning thirst for…"

They were at Anna's shop door now, and Tino thought better of continuing his joke within potential earshot of the progesterone police. They passed the flowers and chocolates, exchanged smiles with the seamstresses and shuffled a few sewing projects around so Hanns would once again have access to the sewing machine he had improvised a repair on the previous morning.

Hanns began to dismantle the machine and Tino pulled up a stool to watch.

"So I'm curious," said Hanns. "What happened to your *Last Supper?*"

"In spite of, or perhaps because of the controversy, a few people did want to buy my painting. Some offered very high prices for it, but I was young and proud. Every time they offered me more money, I was convinced I had something more valuable—more worth hanging on to. I refused to sell.'

'One day, I was approached by a man who wanted to buy my *Last Supper.* He opened a guitar case and handed me a flamenco guitar. It didn't look like much. The *guitarra* was made traditionally of cypress and Spanish cedar. Practically weightless, it had wooden friction pegs instead of gears. The finish was worn; clearly the guitar had been cherished and played for many years—but the sound was magic—like no other I had heard before or have since.'

'The man left with my painting. I have no idea where it is today. I still have *La Guitarra*. I have shown her to many experts and most admit to never having heard its equal, but none have identified its maker. It is not an Esteso, not a Santos Hernandez, not from the House of Ramirez. It has no marks that would connect it to any of the famous *guitarerro familias*. I can only assume it was made by some unknown savant who stumbled on the perfect combination of woods and had an intuitive knack for tapping and shaving the braces, placing them in the perfect positions on the top, and thicknessing the plates to find a perfect compromise between strength, resonance and lightness—an anonymous work of genius that has become part of my very soul."

"I trust I shall have the pleasure of hearing you perform in the same room some time?" inquired Hanns as he opened his attache and began removing tools. He disassembled the linkage arm and after holding the end with the deformed hole up to the light, he fitted the ends of a few bits into it before selecting one and mounting it on an electric hand drill.

"If you will be our guest for dinner this evening, I would be happy to share some of my paintings and let *La Guitarra* sing for you."

"I would be a fool not to accept your invitation, but since I had already planned to invite *you* for dinner, you will have to surrender your kitchen and allow *me* to do the cooking."

"You'll have to ask *el jéfe* about matters concerning the kitchen," suggested Tino, "but you'll hear no objections from me." Tino smiled.

Hanns clamped the linkage arm into a small vice which he had, in-turn, clamped to the sewing table. Squirting a few drops of cutting oil onto the edges of the deformed hole, he enlarged and rounded it with slow, steady pressure. Producing a selection of small, hollow steel rods from a painted metal box, he measured several of them with a caliper, placed a few back in the box and then test-fitted the others to the new hole in the linkage. Selecting two, he measured their inside diameters with the caliper, placed one back in the box, and put his final selection down on his work towel.

"3-1-6 stainless steel!" Hanns held up the piece of metal as if it were platinum or gold and all should pay homage to the precious object. "Virtually indestructible and hard as a teenage boy—it will outlast any other part on the machine...and it's pretty close to a perfect fit."

Hanns measured the thickness of the linkage arm and set it aside on a clean white towel spread over the work surface. Transferring the measurement to the stainless rod, he marked it with a piece of tape, clamped it in the vice and quickly cut off a section to the desired length with a hack saw. He picked up the piece—hot from the friction of the cutting—with a small pair of pliers and held it under the light to ensure sure no saw marks or nicks were visible, and then lightly burnished one edge with a fine, small file. After pausing for a moment to study a small, well-worn brass hammer, he tapped the piece of pipe into the hole in the linkage.

By this time, a few people, including Anna had gathered around to watch him work.

Placing a small buffing pad into the drill, Hanns rubbed a stick of red jeweler's rouge onto it and began to polish the sides of the linkage arm where the work had been done. This was not painting or guitar playing, but it was clear to his onlookers that Hanns approached his work with the pride, intensity, talent and aesthetic sensitivity of any other artist. The drill whined slowly to a stop and Hanns passed the arm around for his audience to inspect.

"All I've done here is put a new hole inside the old

hole," explained Hanns, as if he couldn't understand why anyone would give such a trivial thing any attention at all. "They make this arm out of a cheap metal that wears out, and then they charge you a small fortune for the replacement part...but with a little *Hannsification*, it can be modified to last forever."

Hanns test-fit the linkage pin in the hole, added a tiny dab of grease and reassembled the machine.

"Watch this..."

Hanns moved the setting lever up and down across its range, each setting producing a tiny, precise, well-oiled click.

"Better than new!"

Anna stood behind Hanns and put her arms around his neck. "I do so love a man with tools," she gushed, batting her eyelashes flirtatiously and tossing a playful roll of the eyes at Tino.

"I have one more exhibit before we finish with 'show and tell'," declared Hanns, wiping his tools down with a small rag and placing them neatly back in the attache case beneath the folded white towel, leaving the sewing bench clean of any signs he had ever been there. Pulling his manila envelope from under the bench, he spread a selection of images across the work surface.

American Indians refused to be photographed

because they were afraid the camera would capture their souls. Images such as these inspired such fears. Here was Tino; contemplating, executing a brush stroke at the exact moment of inspiration, perspiring, entranced, intense, composing images in a halo of light under a medusa of black curls. Several people, including Tino teared up. Some silently opened their mouths, but none actually produced a sound. Nobody present questioned overtly whether the images were a manifestation of genius or divine inspiration— or whether these might not be the same things— but everyone felt the presence of something powerful, mysterious and inexplicable.

A small side window in Anna's kitchen overlooked a grassy area with a few trees—not much of a yard, really—but with a park and woodland paths minutes away, the outdoor space was ideal for growing a few vegetables and hanging up laundry to dry. Beyond this was a small fence separating the yard from that of the neighbor's property behind. Fortunately or unfortunately, depending on which forces were winning the battle between nature and technology at any given moment, the window admitted alternatively the sounds of birds in the forest and the echoes of whining transmissions and motorcycles on the distant *autobahn*. As he cooked, Hanns listened to the engines, guessing what vehicles they belonged to.

It was late in the afternoon and Hanns busily cut vegetables and sliced mushrooms. A measured cup of quinoa sat on the counter waiting to be boiled, and a dessert pie of alternatively colored stripes of thinly sliced fruit had been composed in a white porcelain pie plate with a delicate arrangement of strawberry slices on top. Soup simmered on the stove and a large salad of locally-grown greens had been artfully assembled in a glass bowl from ingredients procured at the local farmers' market.

A vehicle strained in the far background and Hanns heard the driver shift down.

Volkswagen? Citröen? Definitely something air-cooled. Nobody would run a Porsche in that condition.

In the Saudi desert, he had been grateful for the privilege of dining at the officers' mess, but even this relative luxury was based almost exclusively on articles frozen, canned or dried in far away places. Typical meals usually consisted of ossified animal flesh smothered in some variety of too-salty sauce to mask the utter blandness, and supplemented with something like canned peas as a weak tribute to having greenery in one's diet. Having returned to Germany, Hanns thoroughly appreciated every aspect of having access to a cornucopia of fresh produce from its selection through its preparation and consumption.

Though hesitant to let his culinary efforts descend to the level of mac-and-cheese, but wasn't above catering to the less-cultured palettes of children. He stirred a small pot of red tomato sauce he had prepared along with colored rotinni pasta for Anna's son.

Transmission is rough. Timing is way off.
Probably a VW.

In the gallery, Tino and Anna were amusing six-year-old Andreas with a board-game that involved arranging words on a grid. Though he received occasional hints from his parents, the boy had a command of language that impressed Hanns who listened and observed passively with the ear that was not focussing on long range engine diagnostics. He had never had any urge to have children and had little experience caring for them, but was always heartened when he saw young people show interest in the world beyond television.

The groaning engine turned off the *bahn* and headed towards the village. Hanns heard it accelerate roughly from its stop at the traffic signal at the far end of town and begin to make its way slowly up the cobblestone spine of roadway that culminated at the small plaza where he now prepared the evening meal.

No. A Citröen. I'll go with the Citröen…not the VW. One of the bigger ones, I think…A 602.

"Tino…"

Hanns thought better of asking Tino to look out the window to indulge his game. Not that Tino wouldn't have been willing to get up and look out over the street, but Hanns doubted he had any ability to distinguish a Citröen from a citrus tree, and reflected that Tino probably didn't live very large in the world of vehicular taxonomy. He looked up but Hanns waved him off with a small gesture, walking over to the front window himself.

"A Citröen 2CV with 602cc engine," Hanns announced.

Anna and Tino didn't look, but smiled at Hanns's boyish eccentricity. Neither of them knew what he was talking about. Most probably, neither of them had even admitted the sound of the gasping engine to the realm of conscious awareness.

With a gnashing of metal gears, a battered red and yellow Citröen camionette—a small truck with square headlights and corrugated side panels—lurched up the street, sputtered agonizingly, fired a few more times and died just below the awning in front of Anna's shop. The driver turned the engine over and over, straining the starter to no avail.

It was just starting to get dark. A figure emerged from the truck, looked briefly at the "CLOSED" sign on Anna's shop door and glanced up at Hanns who looked down from the window above, The man smiled helplessly with upturned palms.

Hanns looked at the clock. "Anna, can you turn the oven off in 15 minutes?"

Anna nodded, noted the time and continued her board game with Andreas.

Tino accompanied him down the stairs.

"*Gracias, señor.* My truck, she…"

"I heard you coming from back on the *bahn*," interrupted Hanns. "I hope you're not planning to go very far with this vehicle?"

"I am go to *España* to make a film of bullfighting and to finish my study of *toreo*. Forgive me…I am Antonio. *Si posible*, may I use your phone?"

"*Soy Tino, y mi amigo es Hanns, pero no hay un taller mecánico aquí que está abierto*," offered Tino, accommodating the stranger in his native language but disconnecting Hanns in the process. Thinking better of this tactic, he continued. "The mechanics are all closed. Come upstairs, have some dinner and we'll see to your truck in the morning. I have a spare bedroom upstairs."

"*Gracias, Señor Tino*, pero I could not accept such hospitality."

"You don't have much choice," said Hanns. "You won't have much luck pushing your truck over the hill to the inn in the next village, and it's already getting dark. I'll take a look at the truck in the morning and see if I can't get you on your way, but from the sound of it, you need more than a tune-up.

Unless you want to sleep in your truck here on the plaza, you should think better of turning down a comfortable bed and a hot meal."

A few drops of cold rain began to fall lightly, one striking Antonio in the middle of the forehead.

He looked down—defeated—and then smiled weakly at Hanns and Tino. "*Gracias*. Thank you. "

"This is a very safe area as far as crime goes," joked Tino. "Let's carry your stuff upstairs and we'll keep it that way."

Antonio opened the back of the truck and together, they muscled three suitcases and a flat wooden crate through the dress shop and up the stairs.

Knowing Tino's hospitable character, Anna had anticipated Antonio's arrival. The salad bowl sat on the low table with a stack of smaller bowls, a water pitcher, glasses and an extra bamboo place mat.

"It's your lucky day," Hanns offered to Antonio as they entered the gallery.

'Antonio, meet Anna. Anna, meet Antonio.'

Anna smiled and bowed her head politely.

They dropped Antonio's suitcases next to Hanns's attache case in a corner of the gallery and leaned the crate against the wall.

"More details later," Hanns explained to Antonio

with mock urgency. "I'm famished. Get washed up and let's get this feast started."

Antonio smiled weakly through the mild shock of adjusting to the new circumstances that had suddenly been thrust upon him, as Hanns ushered him to the washroom.

Hanns poured the red sauce over Andreas's rotinni, placing it on the table before him with a smile and then began filling salad bowls and water glasses.

"It seems," said Hanns to Anna and Tino "that Anna's Magical Accessories for the Dance is attracting all sorts of interesting characters these past two days. Is this a regular thing with you?"

"Here," smiled Anna, "anything and everything unusual is a regular thing."

Tall, awkward and wiry, Antonio appeared to have been assembled with chunks of clay stuck to an armature. One could imagine him bending anywhere along his frame instead of only at the joints. He had the dark features of his Spanish forebears; a fine moustache teased into Daliesque little tips at its ends, and hair slicked back with copious amounts of some sort of gel. In concert with the moustache, a pair of heavy, thick-framed glasses framed his largish nose, and Hanns half-wondered if the glasses might not have originally been purchased with their own exaggerated plastic nose and moustache. Emerging from the lavatory, Antonio had changed into black pants and a white, long-sleeved shirt sporting an almost-feminine ruffle down the column of buttons. Open shirt cuffs were rolled back almost to his elbows.

Sitting cross-legged at the low table, he closed his eyes, folded his hands and began to say grace in Spanish. Tino, Hanns and Anna remained respectfully silent while Andreas explored the possibilities and potentials of printing with rotinni pasta on his white shirt.

Hanns looked at Antonio. "Forgive the intrusion, we don't often have the pleasure of dining with bullfighters. Could you indulge us with a description of your quest?"

Antonio looked caught in the headlights and Tino translated the question.

"Since I am small boy, I am love *el toreo*— bullfighting. I read and I study everything, but *mi familia*, they say I am crazy.' 'Antonio, you going to kill yourself.' So I keep reading and studying but I go to University in Berlin and I study finance. I not like this so good, but is good job—pay good money *en España*.'

'*Pero*…in the summers, *mi familia*, they think I stay and study in University, but I go to *un Escuela de Toromaquia*—a school for *toreo*—for bullfighting. I learn and practice now four years.'

'Now, I have my papers from University and I have certification from *toreo* school. I am go back to Spain, to *Sevilla* to show *mi familia* I am a *torero*.'

'But, *mi fantasía es* to make a film about *el toreo*. In Berlin, I buy a camera. In *España*, I will make a movie of *el mundo de toreo*—the world of bullfighting.'

The evening wore on and the meal was excellent. Tino and Antonio jabbered in Spanish about places they both knew in *Sevilla*. Hanns gathered up empty plates and then cleaned and dried the dishes over Anna's protestations.

"Antonio," offered Hanns. "Not long ago, I was in Saudi Arabia. My job was to shoot films for the Saudi military to document their operations for the King. I did this for a few years, and made some movies I'm quite proud of.'

'I'm also a photographer. Tino can show you some work I brought over just today. Would it be possible to see your camera—if it's not an inconvenience? I'm curious…but I'm also hoping it's in better shape than your car." Hanns smiled.

"I am happy to show you. I know not much about this camera. Maybe, *Señor* Hanns, you will show me how to work it? It is in the big box, if you will help me to open it.'

Hanns and Antonio grabbed the wooden crate and slid it gently onto the floor on its back. About as wide as Hanns's outstretched arms and maybe half as tall, the box was well constructed with brass hinges at the top. Opposite the hinged side was a tiny padlock that might easily have been pried open by a child with a pair of pliers, but which presented at least an illusion of security.

After fumbling in his pocket to produce a tiny key which he twisted in the lock a few times, Antonio snapped open the shackle and raised the lid. Removing an object from white towel wrappings, he proudly presented his camera.

It took him a moment to realize that Hanns and Tino's looks of astonishment were not directed at the battered 8mm camera, but into the box on the floor behind him.

There, wrapped in clear plastic and masking tape, was Tino's *Last Supper*.

"In Berlin, I have a cousin," explained Antonio. "He sells *artes y* antiques. When people die, he buys their things from the *familias* and sells them. He also has a big art gallery in *España*. When I finish at University, he give me some paintings to bring home to *Sevilla*.'

'He tell me, "you like any painting, you keep it for your graduation present." I think maybe I keep this other painting here, but if you like this one, I give him to you for helping me. It is maybe a bit—how you say?—blasphemous—no?'

Tino had tears in his eyes.

Hanns opened his attaché which still sat in the corner, withdrawing his brass hammer, a box of nails, a tape-measure, a pencil and a level. He measured the wall and made a faint mark, tapped the wall to find a stud and drove the nail expertly to the perfect depth with a single blow. Leaving the hammer on the floor, he pulled his knife from his pocket, cut away the plastic wrap and hung *The Last Supper* as if the wall itself had been ordained by God to receive it. Executed more like a ballet than a picture-hanging—each step flowed as if choreographed into the next, culminating in the painting's magical appearance on the wall in the perfect spot.

Anna marvelled at the piece, having never seen Tino's painting before, though she had heard its story.

Hanns adjusted one of the track lights on the ceiling to illuminate the canvas and they stood back, admiring it.

"Do you know," asked Antonio, "who is the artist of this?"

Inspired by the paraphernalia painted in front of Jesus, Tino pantomimed removing a top hat from his head and setting it on an imaginary table. Twirling an imaginary wand briefly, he tapped it on the imaginary upturned hat brim and then grabbed his hair as if lifting himself from it.

"No," said Antonio. "It is not *posible*."

Tino grabbed one of the smaller artworks from the wall, showed the signature to Antonio, and then gestured to the one beneath *The Last Supper*. They were clearly identical.

Antonio crossed himself.

First Hanns, then Tino, and then Anna began to laugh out loud. "*Mi amigo…*" offered Tino to the dumbstruck Antonio. "Forgive us. We are not laughing at you, but you are the one crossing yourself. You should be the first to believe *anything* is possible…and I assure you there is nothing sacrilegious about the painting."

Tino turned to Hanns. "You were telling me God has a sense of humor. Surely, after tonight, we can say so for certain—a very good one, I think."

They stood, studying the remarkable image.

"My cousin," explained Antonio. "He buy this painting a few years ago. A man, he die and his *familia* sell his things fast and cheap. But my cousin like this painting. He keep it in Germany for a few years, and now I bring it home to *Sevilla* for him.'

'I think he no expect me to choose this one, so he not say anything to me, but I give him to you. My cousin always look for who the artist is. He will maybe be mad I give away the painting, but I think it is good business for you when I tell him I find you."

Andreas sat through these proceedings with a patience laudable for a six-year-old but an attention span typical of one. He now politely asked to be released from the adult world to go play in his room. Anna leveraged the request to coerce the lad into brushing his teeth and putting on his pajamas, then kissed him before he tromped up the stairs and out of sight.

After a period of recovery, the group dived

into Hanns's fruit pie, and would have finished it off completely had not Anna's maternal instincts overwhelmed their taste buds and inspired her to reserve a sliver for young Andreas. She made strong coffee for Tino and Antonio, and clinked her water glass against Hanns's.

Hanns inspected Antonio's camera.

"For to make a *documentario* of the bullfight," explained Antonio over his comical glasses. "*Toreo* has history, tradition, fear, valor, conquest, defeat. It is not, as many people think, a fancy way to kill a bull."

Until now, Antonio had been somewhat compressed, like a coil spring wired closed for shipment somewhere. Now, as he spoke of *toreo*, he became animated, his two black caterpillar eyebrows hopping up and down behind his comical glasses.

"Many people say *toreo* is a public execution," Antonio went on, "but they have no problem to go to the *carnicería* and buy a steak. They do not ask how it was the animal died. Did it suffer? Was it afraid? How was it treated when it was alive?'

'My friends, I have been to this place where they kill the animals. It is a very sad thing to see them suffer.'

'In the bullfight, it is true the animal has some pain. I am sorry for this. In life and in death, there is pain. But we do not shoot them in the knees and wait for them to bleed to death. In the slaughterhouse, the bull has no chance. In *toreo*, the bull may win. He may even kill the *torero* or earn *indulti*—a pardon—and not have to fight again. For the bull, it is not a slow death and I think less painful, less fearful than in the house of *matanza* where they kill them for food. In *toreo*, the bulls are cared for, fed well, allowed to exercise. On the farm, some grow up in a tiny space."

Antonio was on his feet at this point, strutting before the gallery window and gesticulating dramatically.

'I plan to make a film—to show that *el mundo de toreo* is a beautiful history, a beautiful tradition, not so cruel as people think.'

'And since I study *toreo*, I am going to fight the bull myself—to be a *torero*."

Antonio beamed proudly, his head tossed back and his eyes closed triumphantly as if imagining dark-haired *señoritas* throwing red roses at his feet and the roar of the crowd at the *Plaza de Toros*.

Hanns inspected the camera, looking through the viewfinder, winding the spring, removing the lens and holding it to the light. "I don't want to be the bearer of bad news, but even if this camera does work properly, it is made to capture birthday parties and high school graduations. The lens has fungus on the coating, has no zoom feature, and mediocre optics either way. 8mm is too small a format for serious film-making.'

'You can make a movie with this, but you won't capture vibrant colors or be able to play with depth–of–field. Your images will not be crisp and you'll have problems with blurriness on fast-action shots.'

'I like your idea and I admire your passion, but the story of *toreo* will require better tools than this."

Antonio looked down, his spring beginning to recompress. His truck was broken and his camera was *mierda*.

Hanns walked over to his jacket hanging on a hook near the door, reached into the inside pocket and returned with a small case. Snapping it open, he removed a pair of aviator's sunglasses. With outstretched thumbs and forefingers, he removed Antonio's Groucho Marx glasses and replaced them with his sunglasses.

"Don't move," said Hanns smoothly but arrestingly, circling Antonio's face. He motioned for Anna and Tino to look at the transformation. "*¿Muy interasante, no?*"

"What is it?" queried Antonio uncomfortably as he tried to shift the attention of his hosts back to *The Last Supper*.

"*¡Que bonito!*" exclaimed Anna.

"Don't be surprised, Antonio, if you wind up getting your picture taken before you leave us," offered Tino. "Hanns is quite the artist with a camera."

"Thank you," responded Hanns. "Regrettably, this particular pair of sunglasses is very special to me and I am unable to summon up a sense of charity sufficient to compel me to part with them, even for this most noble of causes." He replaced Antonio's original glasses back on his head, put his sunglasses in their case and back into their jacket pocket.

"I call these my "force-field" glasses...a little superstition I indulge myself in.'

'Any time something blows up around me—which it invariably does sooner or later—as long as I have the glasses with me, I escape unharmed. Rationally, I know it's just that I've always had the glasses with me when the near misses happen—and I've always escaped—which is why I'm here talking to you. Of course, now that I carry them with me all the time, it's a foregone conclusion that my good luck comes from the glasses...but, for those of us who live life dancing on a wire, small totems like this can certainly do no harm.'

'I do think we should find Antonio a good pair of aviator's glasses, though."

"And now..." announced Tino loudly, seizing the

attention of the room, "If you will follow me up to the studio, I will show you my paintings, unveil my newest—which only Hanns has seen—and then follow up on a promise to play some flamenco guitar."

Anna followed Tino up the stairs. Hanns lagged just behind her where he found the angle of view to be provocative. Focussed as he was on Anna's posterior, he failed to notice Tino frozen in the studio doorway until everyone collided at the top of the stairs.

The next moment happened in agonizing slow motion.

Tino opened his mouth as if to scream, but only a tiny string of soundless saliva emerged, wrapping around his cheek as he began a glacial rush into the room.

He crouched and then launched himself forward, bringing clenched fists downward past his sides and ascending into the air as if suspended on wires.

A halo of light appeared as his black curls wildly obscured the overhead lamp, his knees coming together into his chest as he glided across the room towards an obscure object on the floor.

As the frozen moment continued, Hanns and Anna realized with simultaneous horror that the object was nothing other than Tino's precious *guitarra*.

They strained to shout something, grab the guitar or somehow reach out to Tino and make him stop, but they too, were frozen in time and could only open their mouths helplessly.

In the tiny instant-within-an-instant before Tino's feet came down in unison, Hanns noticed something unusual about the guitar. *Does it have a hole in it?*

Tino landed on the instrument with heels together. The top buckled and collapsed. Fractured pieces of cypress and cedar tumbled weightless in space. The neck and fingerboard rotated and separated, suddenly released from the tension of the strings. The bridge bounced off Tino's boot. An ebony tuning peg towed a thin white spiral of guitar string skyward before hitting the end of its tether and tumbling crazily back. A thin veil of dust and time-suspended wood particles hovered over the imploding instrument.

The scream of the dying guitar was dramatic—sudden—like the death of a living thing—the liberation of a soul. A visceral crunch and the sound of a single note broke the room—or perhaps the sound of all possible notes at once. No fundamental, namable pitch was distinguishable, only a percussive ring followed by a clash of overtones. Harmonics bounced off walls like a blind genie frantically escaping a hot brass lamp, echoing interminably, and finally yielding to a hollow, profound and equally overpowering silence.

Nobody said a word…except Tino who raised a hand to his forehead. "*Muerto*," he said. "Dead. I could not allow either of us suffer."

Time, capsized, righted itself. The hum of the lights became audible. Everyone drew a deep breath. The room came back into focus.

In the shadows, on the floor next to the shattered guitar, with eyes wide like saucers sat Andreas, Hanns's brass hammer still tightly gripped in his trembling hand.

PART II

The Citröen hummed along quietly and smoothly, speeding Southwest and sporting a fresh coat of khaki paint over which, on each side, Tino had carefully hand-lettered in maroon type:

FLAMENCO TOREO FILM ART ENTERPRISES
Magical Images for the Dance

Antonio sat next to Hanns in one of two sports car seats Hanns had installed up front, and Tino reclined sideways behind them watching the French countryside glide by through the side windows. The three had left before first light that morning and were now enjoying a lunch Anna had prepared for them.

"*Señores*, how do you eat the *arroz* from inside—and *is this seaweed?*"

Hanns and Tino laughed and each took a bite from their nori rolls.

Antonio took an uncertain bite of his, chewed tentatively a few times and then vigorously nodded his approval.

"There's hope," chuckled Hanns.

"I thought the folks at French Customs were going to keep us forever," said Tino.

"I can't be certain this has anything to do with it," said Hanns, "but the War only ended twenty-five years ago, and Uncle Adolf didn't exactly endear himself to the French. You never can tell when you're going to run into someone who's still holding a grudge against the Gerries.'

'Also, at the risk of sounding like I'm tooting my own horn (Hanns pressed the button in the middle of the steering wheel and a deafening foghorn-like blast emanated from under the hood), this truck looks a little too good for a young longhair to be driving. Remind me to look for the Barber of Seville when we get to Spain."

"Is everything okay with the papers on the vehicle?" asked Tino.

"Papers?" returned Hanns looking as innocent as possible and then pausing for effect. "Actually, yes… everything's legit."

"One day these guys will get organized, install some technology and actually *do* something. For now, the best they can manage is to act intimidating and see who starts to sweat. Sometimes, they bring out a dog to sniff for dope, but they really have no easy way to check the legitimacy of a license plate, and if something *was* wrong with our German papers, what's it to them? They're just as happy to have us stuffing Francs into French tollbooths.'

'It's a hassle for these guys to start making cross-border phone calls about things that are ultimately someone else's problem—which means I can go on with my life as quietly and anonymously as possible. I'm not running from anything. I just figure I have as much right to enjoy Planet Earth as the tiny little people who carved it up and perpetrated the ridiculous hoax of selling property and creating borders.'

"But *Señor* Hanns," interrupted Antonio. "I have good papers for my truck. You are legal with your papers, no? Why you play with these people? Why you change the numbers on the truck?"

"Frankly, just for the fun of it," Hanns returned. "In a day of driving, we'll pass through three countries with three distinctly different languages and cultures. They've been at each others' throats for centuries but the race to acquire foreign soil by force is falling out of vogue. Times have changed and all the good real estate has already been stolen. Plus, today's international media exposure has made it so you have to take a certain measure of responsibility to care for the people you're oppressing—and that can be rather expensive. Television has become a much more powerful force for converting heathens into mindless check writers than the gun. European powers don't have much left to do but act civilized and pretend to be friends.'

'There's something ironic about these countries that have sent millions of young men off to war. They levy taxes, build roads and tall buildings, great ships, rail systems, satellites and computers. They create massive economies based on nothing more than numbers printed on worthless paper. Incredible—but it's as brilliant as it is stupid.'

'It's all balanced on the tiny tip of the shared belief that a piece of paper with a thousand *deutschmarks* printed on it is worth more than one with a hundred. Neither of them have any nutritional value whatsoever. They can't keep you warm. You can't melt them down and make jewelry from them or put them to any industrial use. Theoretically, the government will exchange your paper for an equivalent value in gold or silver or tin or shit—whatever the standard is these days—but if everyone came in to exchange their paper for tangible goods, the supply of exchange-material (not to mention its value) would get depleted long before the line of people waiting to exchange their currency had been served. Paper money is a lie—and while I'm just as glad I don't have to lug around gold bars—most people seem to believe their money actually has real value.'

'I'm not stupid. I keep my papers in order. Governments can be brutal with people who won't play the game. I'm not trying to start a revolution. As far as I'm concerned, these authorities are just creations of the ignorant people they pretend to serve and they can have each other. I'm here, and not because I'm being forced to stay. I'm using the system. I have paper money in my pocket. I just like to drive around Europe with a custom license plate. Nobody has caught me yet and if they do, my papers are in order. It's not worth it for them to hassle me over a practical joke. Maybe I'll get a ticket. Who cares?"

Hanns gestured out the window at a castle perched atop a small mountain.

"It kept invaders out and villagers safe—maybe for hundreds of years. Probably, some King or Lord or Grand Hoohah and his family were farting through silk shorts under their gold robes up there in those towers until the plague came along or a band of disgruntled peons hammered the pins out of the drawbridge hinges. Today, it's a tourist attraction with electric lights, running water, colorful flags and a shop where you can buy a snow globe or a plastic sword but in its day, its occupants were just as concerned about land and money as their modern equivalents.'

'I just get a laugh out of how with all their technology and bureaucracy, the authorities are still more frustrated with their inability to force someone to cut their hair than they are with their inability to detect a phony license plate traveling on a main highway across Europe. Dinosaurs ruled the Earth for millions of years until tiny mammals evolved who could crawl between their toes and eat their eggs. I'm just enjoying a little yolk on them before the whole chuck wagon falls into the hands of the cockroaches."

"But *Señor* Hanns, you pay taxes? I hope my question is not too personal, but you rebuild my truck. You bring two nice movie cameras for make a documentary. You offer Tino to buy him a new guitar in *España*. It is very nice thing, but…"

"Yes, I pay taxes," interrupted Hanns, "and no there is no problem with you asking. The question is quite natural and my money is all quite legitimate.'

'To start with the tax question, I pay what I have to and get away with what I can. Like anybody else, if I get paid in cash, I put that money in my pocket and keep it off the books. However, I'm not interested in bringing down the system—just in having some fun with it and not getting suckered by it. If I get sick, I'll use the medical system. If I'm hurt, I'll accept the ambulance ride. If someone robs me, I'll have the police come over and dust for prints. Look at this gorgeous road we're on—smooth as glass and it crosses the continent. I'm happy to pay my fair share to live in this particular little slice of human history where we can fly across oceans and drive across Europe with no concerns greater than whether our practical jokes will fly under the Customs officer's radar. Beyond the greed and stupidity, governments have accomplished some remarkable things and I'm not above recognizing that.'

'But to answer your larger question, I made my money working in Saudi Arabia, first as a pilot and then as an official film-maker for the King. I nearly lost my life filming a military engagement caused by an idiotic real estate dispute over a strip of sand dunes and rocks—not so different than the kinds of things people were dying for up on that mountain over there during the middle ages. They paid me well and I gave them good work in return. Frankly, I didn't have very much to spend my money on over there so it piled up.'

'But when you start thinking about how much paper you get in exchange for what you might have to lose, you start thinking about *value* rather than about amounts of money that might as well be imaginary because you're not actively spending any of it. It took a serious injury and my assistant getting his head blown off to make me realize that.'

'About the same time I decided it was time to head home and start digging into life instead of just working and saving for it, some secret documents went missing from the film room. Here I was thinking I was important because someone had given me high security clearance, but really, they just set me up to be the likely suspect. They questioned me once, but friends warned if they came back to question me a second time, the interrogation would culminate in a "trial" out in the desert somewhere.'

'I saw a jeep pull up to the office one morning and a few Saudis with guns went inside. I hid under a tarp in the back of a pickup truck under the desert sun for one very long and uncomfortable day, until some colleagues smuggled me out that night. That trip is a whole different story, but I landed back in Germany with money in my bank account and one of the King's finest and most expensive zoom lenses in my bag."

"You stole…?" interjected Antonio.

"They were going to steal *my life*. They put me in harm's way just to have pictures taken. I'm not saying it was the right thing to do. It's not like I was drafted and forced to work there. I took the risk, but I can't say I feel guilty about it either. I gave them my best work and conducted myself honestly and professionally. Once they decided to kill me over something I hadn't done, I didn't care much for what they thought of my integrity and perhaps selfishly, figured I might as well have something to gain by my escape instead of just something to lose if it failed.'

'So yes, I stole it…but only if you look at it without any context whatsoever…but thanks to the Saudis and our good friends back in Germany over at Zeiss optics, we're going to get shots a lot of film-makers can only dream about. Only the finest is good enough for the King and that's good enough for me."

Antonio was silent but didn't look troubled by Hanns's disclosure.

"A last question, *Señor* Hanns. You help me with my dream to make a film of *toreo*. You help Tino to find a guitar. What is it you want for *you*?"

"I believe," came Tino's voice from the back seat, "Hanns is here for *the dance.*"

Hanns smiled and pulled into the right lane behind a chrome tank truck to allow faster vehicles lined up behind him to pass. Tino studied their odd little Citröen and its unusual occupants in the rounded, mirrored surface of the tank and began to laugh out loud when he noticed the reversed reflection of Hanns's license tag on their own front bumper.

It read "3M TA3."

The sky nibbled an orange, cream-filled popsicle as the highway followed the Mediterranean coast along the South of France and across the Spanish border. The landscape became more rugged. Date palms and signs exhorting tourists to patronize various hotels, beaches and attractions floated by. Through the side windows, Tino watched distant ships on a blue horizon framed by green mountains and red-roofed villages.

Hanns pulled off the highway at an exit marked *Torroella de Montgrí*, and the Citröen began snaking its way towards the sea.

"Smell the salt, boys? Next stop, *l'Estartit*. We'll spend the night with an old friend of mine."

Though the scrub vegetation was kept green by moist sea breezes, it revealed red and beige patches of earth that gave the terrain a dry character. The road, now shrunk to two narrow lanes, curved along a small mountainside as it descended towards the sea.

"Doesn't look much like *Deutschland*, Does it?" Hanns waved a hand through an open window at white-faced facades on narrow streets. *L'Estartit* was a place in transition—a traditional Spanish fishing village that had been largely unchanged for centuries until one day, it woke up to discover that French tourists and SCUBA divers had taken a liking to its beaches.

"Gold rushes are never pretty," suggested Hanns as they passed a badly painted mermaid on a hotel sign. "A lot of natural beauty gets blasted out of the way to make room for profit. Ultimately, it's a means to its own end, and these sell-out towns usually end up paving over everything that made them desirable in the first place. However, we're still early enough to catch *l'Estartit* while it's still worth seeing."

The sun dropped lower in the sky, dripping orange and cream over the landscape as the Citröen purred down narrow streets to a plaza at the bottom. Hanns turned left onto the beach and continued across hard sand at a slower pace between a row of small hotels and shops and a line of double-ended fishing boats hauled up on the beach.

"*Illes Medes*," said Hanns, pointing out Antonio's window at two rocky islands glowing orange with the setting sun. "Close enough to swim to if you're in shape…and full of fish. Great cave diving, too; grouper there the size of a volkswagen."

"*¡Que bonito!*" muttered Antonio.

"Enjoy it while it's here," said Tino. "I've seen what happens to these little towns once they realize tourists bring more money than fish. I think some of these fishing boats have been sitting ashore for a long time."

Hanns continued towards the far end of the beach where a long seawall extended out into the bay to shelter the fishing fleet and a few small yachts at anchor.

He pulled the Citröen under a date palm and then let the engine idle for a moment and speak to him. Satisfied, he turned the ignition key and with a sigh, leaned his head back momentarily against the seat. It had been a long drive.

"Gentlemen," said Hanns, "we have a short walk but it will be best if you open your bags and carry with you only what you need for the night. Our accommodations are comfortable enough, but space is at a premium.'

'I do need to advise you that because we are carrying some rather expensive equipment with us, I've made some provisions to empower the Citröen to resist the intrusions of those whose standards of integrity might be called into question. Initial attempts to force entry will be met with a reaction that's mostly just annoying. A second level of response will likely cost the perpetrator a few fingers, and then there's a third…"

Hanns paused for impact. "Just do me a favor…

if you need something from the truck in the middle of the night, don't be polite. Wake me and ask me to get it for you. Beyond that, you can sleep comfortably knowing your belongings are locked in what may be the most secure place in Europe."

Antonio and Tino followed Hanns out onto the seawall. A few people were walking on its paved top, enjoying the air. A child tossed popcorn to the seagulls, delighting in the swarm of hovering birds that noisily dipped and swerved around him. Fishing boats were tied sterns-to the seawall, some containing dark men who chattered in Spanish as they handled lines and gear.

After a short distance, the seawall jogged right towards a beacon at its end that sat on a round pedestal encircled by a walkway. The orange sky popsicle melted magnificently into a pool of dusky grape; the beacon flickered and came on, and a warm breeze descended from the land mixing uncertainly with the cool sea air.

Almost at the end, Hanns stopped. A few private vessels, mostly sailboats, were tied here beyond the fishing vessels and they now stood behind one of the larger ones.

"Ahoy *Sorcery*!" called Hanns.

"Dieter is an old friend of mine from flight school," he explained. "There's something about sailboats that makes them especially attractive to pilots, and Dieter is no exception. Beauty, eh?"

A hatch slid open and a large dark-skinned man emerged wearing only a pair of blue jeans tied with a rope belt and a pair of sandals fashioned from tire treads. Dieter stepped onto the seawall, embraced Hanns warmly and offered a brilliant white smile of welcome to Tino and Antonio from under a mane of dreadlocks and beads.

"Welcome to the magical world of *Sorcery*. Come aboard…Come aboard."

Hanns and Tino walked confidently across the narrow board extending from the cockpit to the seawall. Antonio tossed his bag over, nearly bouncing it into the water, and then watched his feet nervously as he inched his way across the gangplank, finally taking Dieter's extended hand and making his final step as a clumsy leap onto the aft deck.

"Let me show you gentleman to your quarters first. Then, I imagine you'll be wanting some food and drink?"

His voice had remarkable presence, projecting an aura of warmth and power, unhurried efficiency and quiet intellect.

"I have plenty of bunks aboard," Dieter explained

smoothly in deep, lyrical and resonant tones, taking the men forward to a cabin with two narrow beds. "There are also two bunks in the main salon and another opposite mine in the aft cabin," said Dieter. "I'll let you fight over who gets to be room mates with whom—or I can throw some cushions and blankets on the deck. It's going to be a beautiful night tonight.'

'Plenty of time to decide, though. Toss your bags up forward. Then come back to the main cabin and make yourselves comfortable.'

'Hanns, since your visit is short, I'd love to change the atmosphere a bit. Can I trust you not to overcook this fish while I tend to a few things? I speared it just this afternoon, and it's just right for four people."

"It would be my pleasure," Hanns replied.

Dieter rummaged in a locker and then opened up the galley counter-top, reaching in and producing a tray of ice-filled tumblers which he filled from a jug of *sangría*.

"If you'll accept my apologies for deferring a proper introduction, I'd like to take advantage of what little daylight remains for our brief voyage to *Illes Medes* where we'll have a little more open space and a little less noisy foot traffic on the dock."

Dieter glided up the wooden companionway ladder

and out into the cockpit of the yawl. The clattering of a diesel was heard from beneath the floorboards and after a few clunks and splashes of dock lines, *Sorcery* slid clear of the seawall and pointed her bow out past the beacon.

Tino poked a head up through the companionway. "May we join you in the cockpit?"

"By all means," sang the deep and cheerful voice. "Come topside and enjoy the view."

Tino and Antonio joined Dieter in the wooden cockpit with their drinks and listened to the thrum of the motor as *Sorcery* made her way past the seawall and out into Mediterranean waters. Ten minutes later, he put the engine in idle and walked casually up to the foredeck. A clattering of chains reverberated through the hull and then stopped as the anchor rode ran and snubbed up on a foredeck cleat. Dieter returned to the wheel, let the boat drift back on her anchor until her bow came into the wind, and then put the boat in reverse to set the anchor flukes into the bottom. Returning the throttle to idle and looking around, he felt how the boat rode on her mooring.

"And now for the moment we've all been waiting for…." Dieter pulled on the fuel shutoff, and the diesel's rumbling yielded to a relieved silence punctuated by the comforting sounds of waves lapping against the hull.

Hanns handed plates up through the companionway hatch. "I hope everyone likes their fish *just right*."

The sky was now deepest purple with a sliver of moon hanging over a black sea horizon. Far out over the Mediterranean, exquisite details of clouds were revealed for brief instants by flashes of distant lightning. Details of the *Illes Medes* to *Sorcery*'s stern faded to black and gray as night stole away the last color of the day.

"Excuse me for jumping to boat work before introductions. I wanted us to spend the night at anchor where we could swing with the wind and keep nature's air-conditioning moving through the hatches, but it's always best to approach the rocks before it gets too dark," explained Dieter, his words dancing to an inaudible, distant drum. "I am Dieter Volglas to the world of work and commerce. To my mother, my father and my friends, I am Kalimba.'

'Hanns tells me we have quite an interesting crew aboard *Sorcery* tonight."

"We'll get there," said Hanns, "but at the risk of being flogged as a mutineer, I humbly beg the Captain's indulgence in postponing the evening's gam until after the larboard watch has had their mess."

Kalimba smiled warmly, closed his eyes and bowed to his guests.

Antonio was still dumfounded and even Tino, who normally maintained an appearance of unflappability could not restrain himself from tossing a quizzical look at Hanns. They had awakened in a German dress shop, driven all day across Europe and ended up anchored off the *Costa del Sol* with a man who, by appearances, was as inclined to eat them as serve them a glass of fine wine; but *sangría*, a meal of fresh fish and the light sea breezes conspired with Kalimba's marvelous voice to put down any spirit of doubt or distrust.

Second glasses of *sangría* were accompanied by a dessert Hanns had hastily contrived from raisins, sliced fruits, cinnamon and cous-cous cooked in apple juice with a dash of rum.

Kalimba offered his approval. "Very good. Very good. I see you know how to cook on a boat."

He turned to Antonio, "I understand you plan to kill a charging bull with a sword in front of a stadium full of people?" Hanns and Tino laughed. Kalimba's face made it clear the challenge was offered in the best of spirits.

Antonio paused. He was normally somewhat shy,

but had become comfortable with Hanns's and Tino's eccentricities. He had also had his skids greased with Kalimba's *sangría*. "Since I meet Tino and Hanns," he explained, "there is always this talk of *bailando*—the dance. At first, I no understand, but now I think I can explain this dance.'

'As we grow up and learn our way in the world, we meet many people, we become interested in many things. We learn skills. We express ourselves. Each of us must find his dance and his people to dance with. I watch these two crazy guys—they dance, not sit on the side. Maybe they think I no understand. I no talk much, but I listen. I watch. I dance, too.'

'But I not play *la guitarra* or paint pictures like Tino. I not make good photography or work with machines like Hanns. My *baila* is a real dance.'

'When I dance with the bull, I respect my partner. He is fast. He is strong. He is smart. *El toro* makes me better for to beat him, I must also be strong and fast and smart. Every time I trick the bull and jump out of his way, he learns from me. Maybe next time, he knows which way I am moving and tricks me?'

'*Toreo* is, for many, just an exciting show. They sit in a safe place and watch a man fight against a bull. This has been a tradition in my country for many centuries, but for me, I do not see the people. It is only me and the bull. It is a dance that connects me to other artists of *torero*. It connects me to the bull. It connects me to life and death—to God. I am maybe face my own death, but I am *alive* when I am in the *corrida*.'

'Kalimba, you killed this fish with a spear. You *like* to kill the fish?"

Kalimba paused for a moment. "I love *hunting* the fish. I certainly love *eating* the fish, but the killing is the part I care for least. I always apologize to my fish and try to be grateful it gave up its life for my meal."

Hanns nodded. "I do the same. I love diving, but…"

"So for me it is the same. I no do *toreo* to kill the bull. I love the bull. I am sad to kill the bull. You go in the sea and maybe a shark eats you. Is safer to buy fish at the market, but when you go into the sea, you dance with the fish. You no kill the fish because you hate the fish. A good *torero*, he kills the bull quickly. He does not hate the bull or want for the bull to suffer.'

'Some people talk only of the killing of the bull. For me, it is like talking about the final note of a symphony or the final brush stroke of a painting—a tragic thing because it is the end of the dance, especially for the bull or the fish—but it does not make the dance less beautiful."

The men allowed Antonio's words to drift upwards to where Orion was becoming visible through *Sorcery*'s rigging.

"So how is it," asked Tino after a pause, "that we find ourselves in such an interesting place and in the company of such an unusual host?"

Kalimba crossed his arms and leaned back against the mizzen mast. "My mother was a missionary from Germany—a descendant of slaves on a mission for God. She went to Africa to save her heathen brethren and collided with my father who was a tribal chief and medicine man—a witch doctor. The result of that collision was a lot of rethought faith and philosophy, and one child who was both the product of his passionate parents and something different altogether. They called me Kalimba after the musical instrument.'

'Sierra Leone has had its troubles for a long time. It's early exports were black gold in the form of slaves and later, white gold in the form of diamonds. Survival for my people has always depended on finding a way to help greedy foreigners steal from us. My parents worked hard and we lived a simple life, but for us, books were more important than food. In my house, we were taught that knowledge and faith were the keys to a better life—though faith in *what* was left open.'

'My people worked deep under the ground for nearly nothing to mine diamonds for people who grew rich and fat from our labor. It was hard work with little reward. Naturally, we stole what we could from the people who were stealing from us, but that was very risky business.'

'My mother's passport and a few connections at the consulate provided me with an opportunity to get out, but I still had to access that opportunity through a rather dangerous and uncomfortable six day ride inside a shipping container on a small freighter. It would have been worse had I been caught at sea than if I had been caught in port. Small-time freighter Captains are known to drop stowaways overboard instead of facing the stiff fines and the hassles of smuggling charges. There were a few scary moments, but things went mostly according to plan and I ended up in Germany as Dieter Volglas. Thanks to my mother, I spoke the language and thanks to a bit of moonlighting in the mines, I had a few rocks in my pocket to pave my road with."

Hanns smiled.

"So, I had a small fortune in diamonds, but I had seen what happened to people who got too rich too fast from this white gold. All my life I had wanted the means to dream my own dreams, but thanks to seeds planted by my parents, I knew life could be ironic. All the rich, white men dreamed of going home from Africa some day but they couldn't stop making money. They bought gold and silly things, but though they lived much more comfortably than we Africans did, they were as stuck to the diamonds as the people who went down into the earth every day to dig them up. They were mean, arrogant and clearly afraid of us.'

'In Germany, I had no trouble converting the diamonds to cash, but I invested my money in myself. I got a University education that a black man can't get in Sierra Leone. I learned a few languages, studied science and literature, got a commercial pilot's license and then gave the rest of my fortune to a relief agency to help my people back home. I wanted to build my new life from my own resources and not from any damned rocks.'

'Flying turned out to be what captivated me. I can't say the airlines have been fighting to hire a black pilot with wild dreadlocks, but I've done pretty well running freight and flying charters.'

'Once, I got a chance to fly medicine and supplies to Chad where they were having a famine. When I landed, the Customs agent demanded I pay a huge amount of money for the privilege of making the donation. I tried to explain that I was an African and the medicine was free. He stuck a rifle up my nose and extended his open palm. I got back in the plane and took a few bullets through a wing as I left.'

'I flew low over the first village I could see and kicked the supplies out the cargo door. I don't know how much of it survived the fall, but I realized then that the white man is only part of Africa's problems.'

'I kept flying, saved a small amount of money and finally ran into an American couple in Gibraltar who had sailed *Sorcery* across from the Carolinas. They had horrible weather the entire trip—just bad luck really. The boat performed perfectly well, but the cruise was not the romantic getaway either of them had hoped for. The airport in Gibraltar happens to be right near the marina and a small anchorage they call "the graveyard." I was walking by after a flight, and heard them calling their relatives on a pay phone to report they had survived forty days at sea and couldn't wait to never step on a boat again. I knew nothing about boats, but I offered them what I had and they accepted it without negotiation. The next day, we signed the papers, they stuffed their clothes and belongings into some old sail bags and I took possession of a 57 foot wooden yawl. She still had sails lying all over the deck.'

'Since then, I've done some cruising and learned quite a bit about boats and boating. I get calls to do freight runs and bush pilot trips, and that keeps me just flush enough to rent a dock space and keep the boat taken care of. Granted, I get some funny looks when they see that Dieter Volglas is actually a wild black African, but I can talk the talk and walk the walk…and I'm a damned good pilot. Anyway, my life afloat is a little less rich and glamorous than it might first appear, but what I lack in money, I make up for in time I get to spend…well…to borrow a metaphor…*dancing.*'

'I enjoy my flying. I sail. I dive and fish. I read and study. I play my music. These are my dances and I do them for myself and for my people back home who work so hard for so little. For them, I live not the high life, but the *good* life. Living well is my dance."

Hanns, Antonio and Tino responded to Kalimba's monologue with applause.

"Thank you, friends," said Kalimba. "Tino, I understand you are a fine musician. I have a guitar aboard—a steel string and not with particularly new strings on it—but if you'd be willing to strum a bit…"

Kalimba climbed down the companionway ladder without waiting for an answer, emerging with a

-117-

weathered guitar in one hand and an unusual device in the other.

He handed the guitar to Tino who began to tune it by ear.

"My name is Kalimba so it is only natural I should play one. It's a folk instrument with little metal tines that are played with the thumbs. Some even call it a 'thumb piano.' Mine is a bit unusual; I built it myself and extended the range of the traditional version by a few octaves."

Kalimba laid the instrument across his lap and played a pattern in the lower register. Tino followed him naturally, complementing the melodic bass with an alternating chordal figure played over an open drone string. Hanns quietly brought a kerosene lantern into the cock-pit and hung it from the mizzen mast behind the wheel. Kalimba hummed lower notes beneath the instruments' voices and shuffled his foot rhythmically.

A warm glow, whether from the yellow lantern light or from the *sangría* or possibly from somewhere both inside and all around radiated from the four men and rose like a prayer into the cool night air.

———

In distant Sierra Leone, a teenaged boy crawled from a dark hole in the earth and slipped under a barbed wire fence. Wrapped in a rag, a single raw diamond was stuffed in his pants. He hid in the shadows, making his way slowly and very carefully back to his village. Crossing a muddy ditch, he stole behind a graffiti-covered cinder block wall to allow a pair of headlights to pass. Satisfied the vehicle had moved on and he hadn't been noticed, he crept stealthily back to his family's house.

Against his cautionary instincts, he paused in the doorway.

How strange.

He was sure he had heard the most unusual music on the wind.

Tino and Antonio emerged through the companionway and sat in the cockpit with groggy eyes. Kalimba poured strong coffee into large porcelain mugs. A pair of diving fins landed in the cockpit scupper followed by Hanns who clambered up a wooden boarding ladder from the sea with mask and snorkel in hand.

"Pretty back yard you have," he said to Kalimba.

Hanns stood in the scupper. "Gentlemen, we are forced to make a difficult choice. We can either accept Kalimba's invitation to have a day of sailing with fresh seafood…and diving on the reefs and *turistas* or… we can drive all day to *Sevilla* and spend the day cooped up in the Citröen. I would never put my friends in a position where they might fall by the wayside, so I'm afraid it's the open road for us today.

Tino and Antonio glanced at each other, rose wordlessly in unison and pushed Hanns back over the side into the sea.

All laughed as Hanns reascended the boarding ladder, but the clatter of the diesel and the sound of chains spilling through the hawse pipe into the locker beneath the foredeck soon broke the tranquility of the morning. Minutes later, *Sorcery* rounded the beacon at the end of the seawall and with some expert helmsmanship from Kalimba, glided backwards into her spot. Kalimba grabbed the end of the gangplank with a boathook and swung it from the dock back over to the yawl's taffrail while Hanns assisted with securing lines to the neighboring boats.

Antonio and Tino thanked their host warmly.

"Life on the sea is full of powerful magic," Kalimba responded. "It is always my great pleasure to introduce it to good people who can slow down enough to experience its effects on time.'

'I thank you for some new perspectives on bullfighting, for sharing some excellent music and for not doing an unfortunate fish the all-too-common injustice of overcooking it…but it seems I, too, have a small part to play in this little expedition. I'll be seeing all of you soon enough." Kalimba winked at them over his brilliant white smile.

The men embraced. Kalimba returned to his ship and the others trudged down the seawall back towards the truck.

It was gone.

The four men stood around the spot where the

Citröen had been as if it were still there, yet somehow invisible.

"The bastard used a tow truck," observed Hanns. "See the tracks. Our truck is sitting in an impound lot somewhere."

A few morning joggers came towards them and Hanns addressed them in his best Spanish.

"Duscúlpeme Señores. ¿Conoce dónde está el hospital?"

Their response was not entirely comprehensible to Hanns, but Tino and Antonio understood perfectly; though they half-wondered if Hanns was not having some physiological reaction to the truck's disappearance that required medical attention. Why would he ask for a hospital?

"This way," said Tino, gesturing up the street into *l'Estartit*.

*Gracias Señor*es…*Muchas Gracias.* Hanns thanked the joggers and followed Tino into town at a run. "If nobody's in the hospital, we'll just have to hunt it down. If someone tried to break in, we'll know about it soon enough."

It was an uphill climb and the men arrived tired and sweaty a half-hour later at the door of a small clinic.

After questioning a woman at the front desk, they were led into a room where a fragile looking young man slept uncomfortably in a narrow hospital bed, his arms and face covered with blotches of dark blue ink, his right hand lightly bandaged.

Hanns kicked the bed roughly, and the man woke with a start.

Hanns held out the keys to the Citröen and smiled.

The man crossed his arms and said nothing.

Hanns turned to Tino. "Tell him the discoloration in his skin is nothing compared to the discomfort he'll be feeling in a few days if he doesn't get the antidote to the poison."

Antonio looked horrified.

Tino translated.

The man in the bed turned to look out the window and said nothing.

"Tell him this is his last chance to give our car back without having the *policía* involved."

The man bit his lip and continued to stare out the window.

Hanns pantomimed vigorously scratching himself all over. He made his tongue look large and swollen in his mouth. He covered his eyes with one hand and reached out with the other as if groping in the darkness.

The man's lip began to quiver.

Hanns wheezed, coughed and sputtered and sank

to his knees. He clutched at his throat dramatically and closed his eyes.

The man broke and an avalanche of apologies and directions followed. Tino found the man's keys in the pocket of his jeans which were folded on a chair next to the hospital bed and removed one of them at the man's frantic direction.

Hanns turned wordlessly and gestured for Tino and Antonio to leave the room with him.

"¿El antídoto?" called the man after them. "¿El antídoto?"

Antonio grabbed Hanns's arm. "This man he do a very bad thing to us, but you cannot leave him to suffer and die."

Tino laughed.

"There is no antidote for stupidity," said Hanns. "It's just ink. I've trapped him for a while inside his own very tiny mind. If he's lucky, he'll break out of it."

The man's frantic screams followed them to the door where Tino burst out laughing.

"Hanns, that was one of the worst performances I've ever seen! Brilliant!"

"I always try to cater to my audience."

Even Antonio couldn't suppress a snicker at this point.

A few blocks away, Hanns inserted the key into the lock on a pair of weathered doors behind a whitewashed stucco building. He flipped a light switch prompting a fluorescent fixture hanging from the ceiling to hum annoyingly and spray the room with flickering, jaundiced light. Numerous bicycles and parts, a few outboard motors, a wooden work bench with a smattering of disorganized screwdrivers and wrenches and a half-eaten bag of chips littered the inside. Above the workbench, magazine clippings of girls in swimsuits and a faded polaroid of two little girls were taped to the wall. In the back of the dark room, a refrigerator standing next to an unmade cot cycled noisily. Tino opened it to reveal stale emptiness punctuated by a few small articles wrapped in foil. A battered tow truck and the Citröen, which was none the worse for having been stolen save for some blue spatters and burn marks under the driver's side door handle, were parked next to each other in the center of the room.

Tino spoke. "I know we are already behind schedule, but I'd like to do a little experiment. Can you work with me on something that will seem a little odd at first? I'll explain once we're out of here."

He reached in his pocket, withdrew a small stack of

bills and handed them to Antonio. "Around the corner, I saw a grocery with a *carnicería*. Can you run over and buy a small ham and some bread? Don't blow the bank. Buy a week's worth of groceries—quality stuff—nothing gourmet, but no junk food."

Antonio shrugged his shoulders and slipped out the door.

"Hanns, you're on organizing and cleaning duty. If it's nasty, throw it out. If it's too funky to do anything with, leave it, but let's see what we can do to straighten this place up and put things in order. When you're done, let's change that light fixture overhead. It's easy enough to reach if you stand on the tow truck boom, and we passed a hardware store a few blocks down."

"But Tino," Hanns interrupted…

"I know. Work with me," Tino replied. "We'll hit this place hard and be out of here in less than an hour…I promise. I may be crazy, but I'm not *crazy*."

Hanns smiled and went to work, first moving some of the larger items into some semblance of order and then cleaning with a rag soaked with mineral spirits found under the work bench. Satisfied he'd accomplished something, Hanns slipped out the door just as Antonio returned juggling four big bags of groceries."

"*¡Que bueno!*" he exclaimed, taking in the

transformation. He set about stocking the refrigerator and shelves with food.

In a surprisingly short time, Hanns returned with a new bulb for the refrigerator, cleaning supplies and a new light fixture which he easily installed, somehow managing to introduce only a few seconds of darkness while one fixture was exchanged for the other. He even placed the photo of the two children in a small frame he had purchased and hung it on the wall a distance away from the swimsuit girls.

Hanns found the tow truck's key in the ignition and fired it up. Shutting it down and popping the hood, he removed the distributor cap and cleaned inside it. He started the engine again and in a few moments, had it running more smoothly. "Poor man's tune-up," he explained, shutting down the truck again to avoid filling the room with fumes. "You get what you pay for."

Meanwhile, Tino had gone to work on the outside of the tow truck. In bright red letters with yellow drop shadows on the doors and bumpers, the signs proclaimed:

Hombre Honesto - Remolque.

"Honest Man Towing," explained Tino. "I'm

rebranding him."

Hanns did a fair job removing the stains from the door of the Citröen with the last of the mineral spirits, and a few minutes later, the clean beige truck with its three unusual riders glided back out through the twin barn doors. Hanns stopped to drop the key in the mailbox and a short while later, they were once again speeding down the Spanish coast, riding the drafts of the big trucks and watching the Ocean through the windows.

"There are many ways for a man to interact with the world," proposed Tino.

"The cooperative model encourages people to work together, and help each other. It depends on communication, integrity and a shared awareness that a chain is only as strong as its weakest link. Everyone is interconnected, and the failure of one member can bring about the downfall of all the others. It is about community and society.'

'Then, there is the victim model—those who live off their own helplessness. If people are rewarded for this behavior by living successfully off the sympathy of others, they often become real victims. I knew a man once whose livelihood became dependent upon his bad back never recovering. He lived in a great deal of pain, was convinced the system owed him support and ultimately died in a drunken accident as a fairly young but broken man. People certainly encounter genuinely dire situations, but we hear stories all the time about those who rise above them. Within reasonable limits, helplessness is a learned survival trick, not a natural state.'

'The competitive model divides the world into predators and prey. If you have tools or wit to be a successful predator, you may wind up with a fish dinner or…," Tino looked at Antonio, "…a bull steak, but there is liability here, too. To play in that world, you must submit to the possibility that you will become prey. Maybe a shark will eat you? Maybe, the bull will gore you? Survival of the fittest implies the possible demise of the less-than-fit."

"So where do *you* think our brightly colored thief falls on this spectrum?" asked Hanns. "It seems pretty clear to me he's a predator, though today, he was the one eaten by the shark and gored by the bull."

"That's certainly a part of it," offered Tino, "and according to the rules of that game, to the victor go the spoils. We would have been entirely within our rights to help ourselves to anything of value we found in his junk pile—or to destroy anything we wished him not to have. As a predator himself, *Hombre Honesto* will know this and will expect to come home to find everything in ruins."

'As far as that goes, we already had the joke on him back in the hospital. He's lying in bed waiting to die a horrible death, and sooner or later, he'll realize he got played. He's going to feel pretty stupid…and he'll look funny for a while until he can get all the blue off his face, but he's also going to realize he's not the biggest predator in the sea. We've given him some things to think about."

"But I do not think *Hombre* fits the cooperation category or the victim category," countered Antonio. "He is not a helpful citizen, but he is not collecting loose change on the streets and sleeping in the gutter."

"You are right," said Tino. "But remember what I said about *believing* you are a victim. Look at the decay in *Hombre's* life; the horrible food, the depressing yellow light, all around him things he has taken from others and now must find a way to dispose of without getting caught. That's pressure—and it reinforces the idea that people are after you. People sink to this level because they believe they have been cast out of the chain. *Hombre* cannot invite a respectable woman to his little dump. He does not take care of himself. He is punishing himself for how valueless he perceives himself to be.'

'But he is a young man; strong and capable. He has a tow truck he can make a living with. I have robbed him of his excuses for being a victim. If he falls back into his old ways, he will have nobody to blame.'

'Also, when it comes to predators and prey, we are not sharks or bulls. We humans can choose to use our teeth or horns—or not. Whether or not he *likes* the people who have turned him into prey, he will respect us because we have gotten the better of him—and he will wonder why we didn't exercise our right as the winning predators to make him a victim.'

'Fundamentally, we have removed external blame from the equation. We have demonstrated there is compassion in the world, and that his receiving of it has nothing to do with whether or not he feels deserving of it. Also, he has a new name—if only as a professional persona—and he can choose to wear that name with pride or with shame."

"So, he's a victim as well as a predator, "said Hanns cynically, "but do you really believe a loser like that is going to reform his ways because some benevolent, psychotic strangers put some meat in his fridge, changed his light fixture and painted a new name on his truck?"

"Honestly, no," countered Tino, "but I don't see that as my goal. Like all growing things, he may blossom in his season or he may wither and die without ever flowering. I am simply fertilizing the soil.'

'Many of the problems people face come from simple lack of thinking. He may have another stolen car in the garage by next week. The ham will get eaten. The refrigerator light will blow out one day. He may or may not see the children in the photo again. He may run afoul of someone a little more vengeful than us. Who knows? But for all the things we can't predict or control, I can assure you of one thing; *Hombre Honesto* will think about this incident for the rest of his life. His personal model of how the world works has been broken.'

When I make a painting, I look for people to love it, but I also look for people to hate it.

I don't *like* that they hate it, but it's like dropping an object into water. If you drop a heavy object, waves spread rapidly to all sides. It doesn't matter which side you measure. Anybody will tell you they love something just to be polite. Compliments are often inauthentic. When people say they hate my work, I know they are being honest. If I see big, fast-moving waves on the negative side of the pool, I know with certainty

I have dropped an object with some weight—with some impact—and the laws of physics dictate that waves must also affect the positive side. If I see only inconsequential ripples, I can infer the work has no real mass. It is a feather—fluff. I am not afraid of people hating my work. I'm afraid of people being unaffected by it one way or the other.

'In the case of *Señor Honesto*, I do not know if, when, or whether he will change. What I can tell you for sure is that we just dropped a large rock in his tiny pond. Whether that rock is a stepping stone or a very strange practical joke is entirely up to him."

At 1:30 AM, Hanns navigated the Citröen along the river down the *Paseo de Cristóbal Colón.* He turned right on the *Calle Antonia Díaz* at a corner of the *Corrida de Toros* next to a small, landscaped park where a statue of a *matador* sat frozen under a yellow streetlight awaiting the dawn. Turning left at the *Calle Adriano*, he slowed down to read the address numbers.

A small group of people emerged from a bar and crowded into a blue Fiat. The car's reverse lights illuminated and after what seemed a long interval, it finally relinquished its parking space and motored off into the *Sevillan* night.

The change from smooth highway driving to the stops, starts and turns of the City awakened Tino who wordlessly extended a hand from the back seat and placed it on Hanns's shoulder to thank him for driving, navigating and delivering them successfully to the site of their next adventure.

Hanns shut off the headlights and let the engine idle for a moment before shutting it down.

He reached over to Antonio and shook him gently. *"Pssst. Antonio. Estamos aquí. Estamos en Sevilla."*

Antonio stretched and yawned. "*Espera*…I mean… wait a moment. I go wake my sister."

Antonio walked over to a doorway, pressed a button and exchanged a few words in Spanish over the intercom. A female figure descended the stairs and opened the front door.

Hanns shut down the engine and looked at Tino. "Antonio didn't tell me this place came with built-in entertainment. If they all look like that here, this is going to be an interesting trip." Tino chuckled, and they climbed out and began to grab suitcases from the back of the truck.

Antonio returned from the doorway with the dark-haired young woman, who was still dressed in heels, blouse and mini-skirt from an evening on the town. "I am Veronica, Antonio's twin sister. Welcome to *Sevilla. Bienvenidos.*'

'You boys are lucky. Our family owns this building and the tenants on the third floor moved out a week ago. The apartment is clean, freshly painted and awaiting new tenants who will move in a month from now. The flat has three bedrooms with a kitchen, dining area and living room, and the previous tenants left behind beds, a couch, a dining table and some chairs. I'm afraid that otherwise, it's a little Spartan but the price is right."

"You speak excellent..."

"I studied it at University and then travelled around after graduation," said Veronica, interrupting Hanns. "Let's get you moved upstairs and then we can decide what to do with the rest of this beautiful Saturday night."

Veronica smiled, executing a playful twirl and the men followed her up the stairs.

They made a few more trips to retrieve the boxes of artwork from the truck and soon, bedrooms were chosen and bags distributed.

"And now, I have plans for you," said Veronica. "I'm sure you're tired, but tomorrow is *Domingo*—Sunday. Everything is closed and there is nothing to do but sleep and eat."

Hanns and Tino smiled. Antonio shrugged helplessly, and they followed Veronica back out onto the *Calle Adriano*, turned, and walked past shops, bars and hotels.

"This is a good location for us," noted Hanns. "It's right next to the *Corrida de Toros* and as a larger street with more traffic, I'm hoping it will attract fewer thieves than the small side streets."

"I wouldn't leave my watch on the seat," offered Veronica with a sidelong glance.

"I do have some heavy camera equipment in the truck that would be inconvenient to haul up and down the stairs every day, but if you hear something that sounds like the s/s Lusitania down on the street, that's just the truck warning someone. I'm not worried about anything actually getting stolen, but there's always the possibility some poor bastard will try."

The four turned and entered a small doorway over which a simply-lettered sign read "FLAMENCO."

The inside was dimly-lit. Tables and a bar were the primary features of the room, and next to that room was another with more tables. A larger room behind the front two could be soon through a Moorish arch at the back through which sounds of people singing and clapping rhythm behind a guitarist drifted forward.

Veronica knew many of the people, and her entrance triggered a flurry of hugs and kissing of cheeks.

"¡*Antonio!*" A pair of arms appeared from the crowd and encircled Antonio from behind. He turned, embracing a busty young woman with dyed-cinnamon hair and a colorful scarf around her neck. They began to chatter away in Spanish, Antonio looking awake and alive for the first time that evening.

Veronica grabbed a round table in the second room where it was quieter and motioned for a bottle of wine.

"Hanns and Tino, meet Vanessa," said Antonio. "She speak mostly Spanish."

Vanessa smiled politely at Hanns and Tino and then looked down at her chair to adjust her trajectory into it, Veronica stealing the moment to roll her eyes cynically.

Antonio held court over the table in his native tongue, recounting the story of how he had broken down in front of the home of the artist who had painted his cousin's mysterious painting, of the destruction of Tino's guitar, of the night aboard *Sorcery* with Kalimba and the recovery of the Citröen after it had been stolen.

Tino listened intently, interjecting a few details in Spanish while Hanns sipped a glass of wine and followed as best he could.

"And now I wish to share *un secreto*." Antonio paused and raised his glass to the others at the table.

The details of Antonio's proclamation delivered in Spanish are herewith translated.

"For four years, I have been in Berlin completing my studies in finance and business—an endeavor I have pursued with determination if not with any great conviction—and I have returned having successfully obtained a degree and certification in my subject...but during week-ends and summers, I have been pursuing an entirely different *métier*.'

'I am proud to announce that I am ready to do what I have always dreamed of—to become a *matador*."

Vanessa clapped enthusiastically and hugged Antonio. Hanns and Tino raised their glasses in support of their friend's proclamation. Veronica crossed her arms and looked stormily at her brother through dark, Spanish eyes. "What the hell is it with you and this need to destroy intelligent animals at a public execution? I just don't get it!"

"Vero…"

"No! *Toreo* is a cruel thing. You take a poor animal, throw it in front of a crowd of people where it's scared half out of its wits, stick it full of spears while it tries to maim a bunch of defenseless horses, dance around it with a cape until you've finished toying with it and then plunge a sword into its heart.'

'You call this a sport? Just because the animal is intelligent enough to qualify as a real adversary and possibly fast and strong enough to put a horn through your chest? I pit my life against the Spanish highways every day along with idiot drivers who are at least half as smart as a bull—and twice as dangerous behind a wheel—but I don't think of commuting as a sport just because there's a fair chance I'll get killed every day and the roads have crosses all over them to prove it."

Antonio stood up and leaned over the table. "Why is it everybody thinks bullfighting is about killing the bull? The killing of the bull is the final part of an elegant dance, the final note of a symphony by which it is unfair to judge either the performance or the composition.'

'I am never glad to see the bull suffer or die, but I am grateful to see the *matador* survive the contest. It is very frustrating for the *torero* to have his painting disappear at the moment of the final brush stroke, but it makes the painting no less beautiful. You..."

Veronica interrupted. "A symphony does not care if it is played or not. A canvas does not suffer if the art is poorly or tastelessly executed. You cannot compare an inanimate note or a brush stroke to a bull who has no choice but to perform at his own execution."

Hanns raised his glass. "A toast to people with dreams and opinions," he said. "I am here at Antonio's request to make a documentary about *toreo*—but this does not mean I am here to make a film either in favor of bullfighting or against it. It means I am here to document it as honestly and objectively as I can."

Hanns paused and gestured for Tino to translate for anyone who did not understand him.

"All arguments and opinions are important parts of

the story, but here's rule number one…." Hanns looked at everyone to make sure he had their attention. "If you say it and I don't have a camera pointed at you, *you never said it.* On Monday, we will visit a bull ranch and we will have an opportunity to start forming fact-based opinions about these animals and how they are treated.'

'If all interested parties can agree to call a truce during this evidence-gathering period, we can explore the subject of *toreo* honestly and without the need for conflict."

Hanns paused again. "Who's in?"

Veronica was still smoldering and Antonio was in no better shape, but each nodded their assent. They ultimately exchanged guarded smiles, reconciling in that way only siblings can. Vanessa clung to Antonio's arm and leaned her head on his shoulder.

Tino quickly abandoned the table for the music in the back room, and soon managed to put his hands on a guitar. A circle of people clapped and shouted with powerful intensity, driven to a frenzy around a twirling dancer. Hanns, Antonio, Veronica, and Vanessa crowded into the doorway and watched Tino dominate the tiny instrument in a transcendental fury, occasionally gasping or shouting as the spirit of the music carried him and his listeners to faraway places and times long past, across oceans and deserts, glaciers, jungles, prairies and sun-drenched beaches.

Veronica whispered in Hanns's ear, "Am I imagining things or is Tino glowing?"

And indeed, it was difficult to tell if Tino was actually radiating some form of energy, or if it was just some trick of the lights filtered through the smoke in the room.

The piece ended with a shout from Tino followed by a leaden silence. The dancer fell dramatically to the floor. After an awkward pause, a girl on the far side of the room finally thought to clap, bringing the others out of their collective stupor and triggering a spirited ovation.

Hanns placed his empty wine glass on a tray and nodded at Tino who didn't see him. He had already begun a passionate *legato* introduction to the next tune and had the dancer quivering to her feet like a marionette waking from a coma.

The sky turned from black to purple to pink before the music stopped.

Hanns awoke with a head resting on his shoulder. Light streamed through the window, and he felt the warmth of a body against his own.

"Good morning. That was quite a performance last night."

Hanns cleared his throat. "You know, that was actually the first time I've gotten to hear Tino play except for one time informally at…"

Veronica chuckled. "I was talking about you. Bravo! Very sweet."

Hanns smiled and then suddenly raised his eyebrows. "Where's Antonio? Is he going to be angry that I…"

"Banged his sister?" laughed Veronica. "He probably wouldn't be too happy about the idea, but Antonio sleeps like he's dead. He's always been that way. A lot of life has gone by in the next bedroom while Antonio blissfully dreams about his world of virtue and everlasting reward…so we can lie here. You'll hear him babbling in his sleep about 15 minutes before he actually wakes up, and we were out pretty late last night. I expect he'll be out for quite a while longer."

Hanns cleared his throat quietly. "So, tell me then about Antonio's 'world of virtue.' Also, I think you had something to say about the girl with the scarf and the big…"

"Vanessa," interrupted Veronica. "She's been trying to drag Antonio into bed for years. They're the irresistible force and the immovable object—drawn to each other but always driving each other crazy. Whenever they see each other, it usually ends up in some sort of scene where they vow never to speak again—but it never works out that way."

"So why wouldn't he jump in bed with her? What's the big deal?"

"Antonio is very into his Catholic values. He's one of those rare people who is actually saving himself for marriage. He'll be bummed out for two days over having slept-in instead of going to mass this morning."

"So hasn't he ever…?"

"I don't think so. He has a very biblical sense of morality. Vanessa thinks she's the hottest thing in *Sevilla* and she's used to having guys throw themselves at her. Frankly, she's used to catching a lot of them when they do…though that's not really my objection. Antonio brings her roses, takes her out for a nice dinner, shares a bottle of wine with her and then leaves her at the door of her flat. It drives her crazy, but I think she likes it, too—which also drives her crazy. A little old-fashioned respect can be a charming thing. There just comes a time in a relationship when tearing someone's clothes off isn't so disrespectful."

"And at what point in a relationship do you think that should happen?" chuckled Hanns, sliding a hand around the contour of Veronica's hip?"

Hanns felt a hand move up the inside of his thigh. "It really depends on the relationship.'

'We live in a Catholic country. We are raised with Catholic ideals—but for many people, the threat of hell and the reward of heaven seem distant, faraway… and frankly, a little fantastic if you take them literally. I can believe in heaven and hell, but I think of them as states of being. One can experience a tremendous sense of joy, peace and wellness or a crippling sense of anxiety and despair. Few physical experiences can match the intensity of these emotional, spiritual states—which makes me question the fires of hell as much as all of that wings, harps and halos stuff. I mean, think about it; if you're *good* for your whole life, when you die, you have to float around in the clouds with a robe on forever?'

'Then there's all that exclusivity stuff. Muslims and

Jews can't come in. Does heaven have a special ghetto for 'good gypsies?' It doesn't seem very compassionate or forgiving to me.'

'Morality isn't based on much if its principles are simply prescribed by God's owner's handbook; a book of dubious authorship that's been translated and rewritten a hundred times. That might be great for people who don't want to have to think about their places in society—and in the world—but biblical morality hardly encourages people to think for themselves. Sure, the bible's full of nice little parables, but people run around wielding these things like little moral hickory sticks, trying to get everyone else to behave instead of just quietly pondering the meanings of the stories."

"You sound like you've taken a few philosophy classes?" poked Hanns.

"A few, but mostly, I got taken to mass every Sunday and forced to attend Sunday school. I had an argument with a priest about the transubstantiation where he tried to convince me that the wine and the wafer actually, *physically* changed into the blood and flesh of Christ after they were swallowed. I stuck my finger down my throat and yacked my cracker up on the desk—which got me kicked out of Sunday school and as far as rational thinking goes, provoked only an explanation that communion is a very sincere form of prayer that didn't work in my case because I didn't mean it.'

'If we have to engage in ritual cannibalism, I guess I'm just as happy it takes place in symbolic form. Less harm is done in chewing a few biscuits than in nibbling on the flesh of a sacrificed person, but spiritually and psychologically, it's not so different than sacrificing an animal. That practice is certainly more socially acceptable to me—animals are routinely killed and eaten—but making a big party out of it is what creeps me out about Antonio and his bullfighting.'

'As for religious practice, it dawned on me by the time I was twelve or thirteen that it lives in a nice little fairy land protected by a high-wall of flawed logic. If it can't be proven or disproven, it's just as easy and reasonable to believe it's true as not. I suppose it's all very comforting for some, but it doesn't hold up very well under any kind of rational inspection."

"Which is great for both of us," said Hanns caressing his bedmate, "because it frees us to share the sheets without feeling like we've got to go run off and confess some imagined sin or be damned to hell for eternity. I suppose forgiveness implies one must be guilty of something, but the only thing I can confess to is not feeling any regrets.'

'But I'm curious. Where do you personally live, Veronica, in the world of spirituality and religion?"

"I'm an atheist. It's not very romantic or mysterious, I suppose, but I believe it's just you and the cold, hard world. You're born, you live, you die and go back to dust. That's admittedly a little bleak for many people's tastes, and that makes the religious perspective a lot more palatable. Unfortunately, it doesn't really make it any more *believable*.'

'How about you, Hanns?"

"Because it's my nature, and whether or not I actually believe in the devil, which, for the record, I don't, I'll play his advocate in our discussion here.'

'I am not a *theist*—meaning I don't believe *per se* in a single, intelligent, omnipotent force that makes rules, demands sacrifices and rituals and metes out punishment. In that sense, I suppose I'm an *a*-theist, but that's a loaded label.'

'There are also agnostics to whom I'll give credit for open-mindedness but who seem to have adopted a label for an empty jar with the top taken off. Declaring openness is a good start, but it doesn't make any sort of statement about having observed any kind of patterns or order in the Universe. One could be a rational pragmatist hoping to see some evidence of the existence of a deity, or one could be a devout religious practitioner ready to abandon all the silly ritual and guilt if only some definitive proof could be found that no God would consider that a punishable offense. Either individual could call themselves "agnostic" but that label says very little about actual spiritual practice or belief. It's a convenient, conceptual carrying handle that can't support much weight.'

'The world is composed of things you know and things you don't know—and also of things you *don't know* you don't know. I'll start there if you're on-board with that premise. The concept of a belief system is somewhat flawed to begin with as it, by its very nature, must omit anything in the third—and largest, by the way—category. Are you with me?"

"I think so. You're questioning the whole concept of belief?"

"Somewhat. It's very limiting and short-sighted to live on planet Earth for a few decades and settle on hard and fast conclusions about how and why things work. The world of mathematically quantifiable things is pretty solid for practical purposes but when it comes to the world of magic and meaning, there's a lot we don't know and quite a lot we don't even *know* we don't know. I'm just saying I'm not going to give you a nice, gift-wrapped picture of the Universe all tied up with a pretty bow and a card that says "wish you were here." Belief systems can be very comforting, as can be adopting a community of people who share that belief system, but they prevent a lot of us from ultimately exploring or experiencing the meaning and the mystery—what a friend of mine would call the 'essential absurdities.'"

"So do you have a name for this belief in not having a belief system, Hanns?"

"I suppose I'm an antinomenclaturist," chuckled Hanns, "but while many people seek comfort in knowing the answers, I find joy in discovering meaningful questions. I suppose I have a certain faith that on some level, the Universe does have a rational order. As an engineer, I deal with numerical prediction systems, and cause and effect. As a thinking being, I rationally carve the Universe up into labeled bits and pieces that I can manipulate according to those systems. Most of my fellow beings share this ability and carve the World up in similar ways. Even a dog can recognize a toy as his own and separate from other objects.'

'Philosophical arguments suggest rational inquiry itself can only stand on the shoulders of an entirely illusory picture of the world, but whether that's true or not, I find a lot of meaning in questioning and exploring that would be utterly ruined if someone handed me an answer sheet."

"I like that," said Veronica. "You're a seeker."

"I was trying not to put a name on it, actually. I just *am*."

"But I'm not sure I get what you mean about rational inquiry being illusory."

"Philosophy can be a lot of fun until it collapses under its own weight. Rational inquiry can only function as long as it has some sort of ultimate reality to support it. It requires one to sustain a picture of one's self as an individual who is making an inquiry about a whole that one may be an inseparable part of—which is contradictory. It also depends on overlooking any deep questioning about reality itself.'

'Every belief stands on a premise which stands on a premise which stands on a premise and so on. If you inspect these ladder rungs to see if they can really take the weight, you'll find the lofty heights of belief to be an unstable proposition.'

'Do you believe in the concept of time, Veronica? I'll warn you in advance, it's a trick question."

"The past is a recorded memory. Reality happens

in the now."

"Good! Spoken like a true student of Zen; a wonderful and philosophically well-fortified retreat for many expatriates from traditional Western religion. I get a lot out of it myself, though I think many of its practitioners fall into the same traps as their Western counterparts. A spiritual *state* is no less abstract than a spiritual *being*, and many people substitute unattainable enlightenment for unattainable God…but we spoke of reality and the *now*….'

'Do you remember your basic chemistry from high school, Veronica?"

"I can't say I'd feel too comfortable if I had to work out chemical equations, but I recall the basics."

"So, if we look at an atom, you recall it has a cloud of electrons whizzing in orbit around its nucleus?"

"Neutrons and protons on the inside and tiny electrons flying around it. I remember."

"But if time is an illusion, the electrons are not really in motion are they?"

"No. They exist in one place in one instant."

"But if you stop all motion, if you freeze it to zero degrees Kelvin, what happens to matter?"

"It falls apart."

"So without time, nothing can exist. Everything

disintegrates into fundamental particles and energy. Either existence depends on prior existence—which we've defined as illusory because it's time-based—or existence itself is an abstract concept we have created to build further abstractions upon. Reality itself is a very fine-grained thing. I suspect if there is any ultimate, external, non-human-thought version of it, only the boulder-sized chunks of it are readily caught in the sieve of human inquiry.'

'Where I'm going with this is that we all take our belief systems way too seriously. Seeking answers is a wonderful pursuit, but the human mind is uniquely unqualified to form conclusions. Belief itself is a form of ignorance. How's that for a Zen paradox?"

"But Hanns, at the risk of inspiring another enjoyable, yet philosophically complex response, you did refer to 'the meaning and the magic.' I'm sure it's not safe to assume you believe in anything in particular, but I'm sensing some spiritual foundation to your world. I'm not going to let you retreat into the temple of Zen paradox so easily."

"Nor should you. I appreciate the challenge.'

'It was you who spoke of heaven and hell as states of mind. I tried opium once and experienced states of bliss that are rationally incomprehensible. I would never do it again as I can understand why people have happily starved to death puffing on an opium pipe. Maybe you've been in love a time or two in your life? I *know* you've had an orgasm or three. It may be that it's an entirely chemical thing and the meaning of life has more to do with endorphins in the brain than with anything truly spiritual or other-worldly, but illusory or not, I have the human capacity to experience happiness—and even to experience happiness vicariously by bringing it to others. I also have the ability to feel pain through being directly hurt, through being neglected or through sympathizing with the pain of others. I don't know exactly *what* this says about the nature of human experience or human interconnectedness, but I'm fairly confident it says *something*. I'm also fairly confident that if I could find a piece of that *something* and put it in a specimen jar, I wouldn't have in there what I thought I had in there.'

'I have experienced amazing instances in my life of the right people showing up at the right times. So many times, I should have been killed but walked away unharmed. You heard the story of Tino's painting? That's the tip of the iceberg. I don't know if an intelligent, compassionate force is taking care of me or not—or if that force exists, if it's external, part of collective humanity or a manifestation of some unidentifiable human capacity for magic, but regardless, I feel like the magic in my life is on my side. It's not punishing me for not attending church or failing to join any particular club. I don't know if or what God is, but we're cool with each other without having to be on a first-name basis. Hell, I haven't been in *Sevilla* for twenty-four hours and I've already got a beautiful woman in my bed. *Something's* looking out for me!"

Veronica smiled coyly.

"I live in a world I don't want to form too many hard and fast conclusions about," continued Hanns. "I'd rather form new theories every day and hang on to my ability to laugh whenever some new experience knocks them over like a child's wooden blocks that get toppled to make way for the next, bigger, better and more elaborate piece of construction. As an active rational explorer, I take comfort in having a bigger bucket than most people of things I know. That comes from joyfully swimming in the vast ocean of things I *don't* know. As for the things I *don't know* I don't know, I'm glad they're out there to pop up unexpectedly and keep me engaged in the game of reconciling the first two.'

'Am I an atheist? A spiritualist? A Zen Buddhist?

A rationalist? Yes. No. Maybe. Only on Wednesdays. I'm not sure these are ultimately questions that truly have much to do with the ascent of man…or the ascent of Hanns if you know what I mean."

"But, Hanns, how do you feel about Antonio and all of his religious concepts of virtue? The lunatic has a shrine to *La Macarena*, the patron saint of *toreros* in his room. I personally just wish he'd get laid and not concern himself so much with the afterlife."

"My biggest beef with religion in general is that so many of its advocates are convinced their answer should be everybody's answer and their book should be everybody's book. Historically, Catholics have tried to forcibly convert just about everybody to their way of thinking and believing—and how's that for a concept; *forcing* somebody to *believe* something?—but the crusades have been over for a few centuries and unlike some other branches of Christianity I've had to personally fend off, contemporary Catholics seem more concerned about their own beliefs than with mine—which earns them a lot more of my respect than I offer most religions. Antonio's beliefs look as much like symbolic, ritual psycho-mumbo-jumbo to me as they do to you, but he's not asking me to adopt them. It may be that if he believes he's protected by *La Macaroni* in the bullring, it's no different than me having a sense of being protected by the strange magic in my life. He's got a label for his magic and I don't. Maybe that makes me more open on some level to deeper questioning and exploration, but in the grand scheme of things, I don't think it'll bring either one of us practically closer than the other to truly understanding the mystery or gaining any kind of ultimate reward.'

'At the risk of shooting down your very genuine and sincere concern, Veronica, you should get laid yourself and not concern yourself so much with Antonio's spiritual life."

"I can't disagree with you. It's just difficult to watch sometimes.'

'So, Hanns, would you care to engage in a little more sin, then…before Jesus wakes up?"

Hanns grinned boyishly. "Not me; I'm far too virtuous for that. What I really like in the morning is just to be held."

Tino knocked on the shop door. Keys jingled in locks and Hanns followed Tino through a green wooden door.

"Soy Tino, y mi amigo, Hanns. Gracias, Señor Ortega. Estamos agradecidos por…"

The fat little man looked at Hanns and interrupted.

"I speak English *y Deutsch*, too for your friend, and after hearing you play last night, Tino, I am honored to open my door for you on a Sunday…provided it's not too early.'

'I am Juan Ortega. I think you will enjoy my collection."

Señor Ortega had made some effort to clean up for his guests but hadn't quite erased the patina of Saturday night. His white button-up shirt was clean but not particularly well tucked-in, and Friday's gray stubble on his neck and chin had not completed its wait for Monday morning erasure.

Juan locked the door behind them, and Hanns and Tino followed him to the back of the narrow room.

"I'll leave the lights out up front and lock the door," Juan explained. "There is the business of selling music equipment which takes place up front there…and then there is the pastime of experiencing fine musical instruments which takes place back here in my "wine cellar."'

'If I leave the shop open, the place will soon fill up with young boys wanting to wank on the stratocasters and blow the windows out with the amplifiers. It's a good business, but it caters more often than not to those who imagine themselves up on the big stage under the lights than to those who actually have that opportunity. I do have a few professional customers, but they usually try to come in at a time when the kids are in school. In any case, one can only handle so much racket in one week. Sunday is sanctuary day."

On either side of an aisle, glass cases offered strings, pickups, audio-effects boxes, capos and other guitar paraphernalia. A rack of guitar straps in various colored leathers, zebra stripes, leopard spots and camouflage patterns stood to one side. Behind the cases hung rows of instruments—electric guitars on one side glistening with candy-colored splendor—and acoustic guitars on the other—a mute symphony of earth-tones hanging in the dim light of the store.

At the back of the room, Juan unlocked another door between two arrays of amplifiers and flipped on the light.

"Tino," queried Juan. "I know you *play* guitar… but how much do you really *know* about guitars?"

Tino shrugged and looked at the rows of acoustic guitars around him. "Honestly, I know what I hear."

"We'll see about that in a minute. Few people really do know what they hear. Let me explain to you this business of fine guitars."

Hanns and Tino nodded their interest and breathed in the smell of woods gathered from around the world.

"Most of the instruments in the front of my store are factory-built instruments. They vary in quality from pretty-good to excellent, but are assembled mostly from machine-made parts. It is the luck of the draw whether you get an instrument made from parts that get along musically or not. Electric guitars are more forgiving, but an experienced player knows that the electric guitar that sounds best amplified is usually the one that sounds best acoustically—if you can listen to it in a room quiet enough to hear it—but let us confine our discussion to acoustic guitars.'

'There is a fairly standard range of woods used to make acoustic guitars. Rosewoods, maple and mahogany are typical body woods—but no two pieces of wood, even from the same species or even from the same tree are ever the same. They are like fingerprints. In a guitar factory, it is necessary to plan around mass production, which means every piece is machined to the same, exact dimensions whether it is from stiffer or more flexible wood stock.'

'A manufacturer must err on the side of building a stronger guitar. The strings on a guitar exert quite a bit of pressure, and wood is fundamentally a plastic substance. You have seen floor timbers—even very large ones—in old houses that have bowed with time?"

Hanns and Tino nodded.

"A guitar is slowly folding in half from the day it is first strung up. It may take ten years or it may take two hundred, but time and tension will inevitably warp the wood. If the guitar is built too stiffly, it will resist the pressure for a longer time—hopefully until the warranty runs out…," Juan smiled, "but it will not vibrate as freely as a lightly-built guitar."

Juan grabbed an old guitar leaning against the wall in the corner and offered it to his guests for inspection.

"Do you see how the bridge is leaning forward, how the top has pulled up and how the strings are high above the fingerboard? This is a steel-string guitar, under more tension and built too lightly. You see what happens?"

Hanns sighted across the guitar's top from side-to-side, measuring the angle and severity of warpage with his engineer's eye.

"A batch of factory-built guitars usually includes mostly 'pretty-good' guitars, a few duds and sometimes a few that sound and play much better than they should. It all depends on what lucky pieces of wood end up in a particular instrument. Do they sing together well, or do they not like each other? Many aspects of guitar-making are mysterious. Sometimes a cheap guitar of industrial quality will have a remarkable voice and occasionally, a piece of art hand-crafted from the finest woods will never sing well.'

'But forgive my being romantic; musical instruments are one of the few inanimate objects that can be said to have a soul, and consequently, they are much like people. Most are "factory-built," and with some love and encouragement can sing reasonably well. A few cannot sing at all, and a few are gifted with wonderful voices. But just like people, even the fat and ugly usually find someone to love them."

Juan patted his belly and smiled. "Some will buy a guitar because it is blue. Some prefer a particular brand name. Some people like the look of maple or rosewood, or want to play the same instrument as a musician they admire. People learn and grow through these instruments.'

'Remember your first girlfriends; the ones you desired so desperately with the passion and naivety of youth? I think we are all grateful today to have moved on from those girls who were at least as crazy as we were, but they helped us to define our tastes and guide our choices. As with love, you may go through many partners before you learn what your heart really wants and as with love, choosing an instrument is a process of learning to listen instead of just look.'

'You spoke of knowing what you hear? People usually don't know what they hear. They hear what they know."

Juan grabbed a guitar off the wall. The instrument was covered with ornately-inlaid mother of pearl and abalone. Up the neck crept an abalone vine with delicately engraved veins on the leaves. He played a chord.

"*Mierda*...This guitar is beautifully crafted but it cannot sing. Some deaf person with a lot of money will be ignorant enough to believe it sounds as good as it looks—and that will be a good day for Juan who is in the guitar business—but I would not open my doors on a Sunday for him.'

'But above the swirling clouds of brand names and advertising and musical soul-searching that is the world of factory-made instruments, there is the world of the hand-built guitar which is to the factory-made guitar as wine is to grape juice.'

'The luthier—the maker of fine guitars—will spend many hours choosing the right pieces of wood for an individual instrument. Every piece is inspected, tapped and listened to, and flexed. Then, if chosen for an instrument, it is tapped and shaved and flexed, and tapped and shaved and flexed again until it has the perfect balance of stiffness and resonance, strength and tone—and maybe some other qualities we cannot name. Every part of the instrument is a one-in-a-thousand piece from a one-in-a-thousand tree.'

'The experience of the luthier is also important. After he has made at least a hundred guitars, like a great player, he will develop a *toque*—a touch. He will have experimented with making certain parts a little thicker or a little thinner. He will have shifted the braces around and will understand how small changes affect tone, and he will understand how to manipulate these things to compensate for a box that is too bright or too boomy.'

'Such guitars are often the ones a real *tocaor* leaves at home. Their finer qualities cannot always be heard in a crowded room or through a microphone and speakers. Many players are just as happy to take an instrument on-stage that can be replaced easily or fitted and refitted with the latest electronics. A good factory-made guitar has its place, but when it comes to the intimate concert or the recording session, or just a practice session by yourself where the voice of the instrument must be inspiring and transporting, the hand-built guitar is the only option."

Hanns and Tino looked around the room again with new perspective. The smells of the cedar tops of the guitars on the wall—like a new box of pencils—and the still-new finishes of lacquer and varnish, inspired visions of white-aproned men in wood-floored rooms sanding and shaving, tapping and listening over workbenches covered with clamps and chisels.

"The flamenco guitar is a uniquely Spanish thing," continued Juan. "It is much like a classical guitar in that it uses gut or nylon strings. It has the same dimensions and similar construction—but is designed for a different musical purpose from different musical materials.'

'A musical note is a complex thing containing an initial attack, followed by an initial decay and then a period of sustain during which the note will die away."

Juan drew a graph in the air with a quick peak and a

gradually fading plateau—like a human heartbeat.

"Though we might hear it as one individual note, we react to the voices of all these parts. The attack and the transition into the sustain are responsible for why most people describe a guitar as being "bright" or "punchy" or "dull." Essentially, there is the sound of the string being plucked that precedes the sound of it ringing. The sustain of an individual note may have subtle character like a fine wine that lingers on the tongue after you have swallowed it, but when you have many notes sustaining at the same time, complex things happen. Every note is made up of other notes—harmonics—and these will combine or cancel each other depending on the way the instrument resonates, the age of the strings, the touch of the player and the mood of God.'

'A classical guitar is made from heavier woods that ring like a bell—woods that add to the quality and duration of the sustain. The neck is also heavier to promote sustain—a desirable quality for most kinds of music. But flamenco is percussive music often played very quickly. If so many notes were to sustain and run together, the music would become brash and cacophonous, so flamenco guitars are built lightly. Unlike other guitars, the body is often made from cypress and the neck from Spanish cedar. These instruments are very light, bright, loud, and percussive. The notes do not sustain much and it is up to the *tocaor* to keep the music moving though the notes may die away more quickly.'

'Cypress guitars are called *blancas* though some *flamencos* prefer the sound of a *negra;* a guitar made from darker, denser woods that is a small step closer to a classical guitar.'

'Fine flamenco guitars are mostly made here in the South of Spain, though more and more people have studied the art of flamenco lutherie and taken it to other places. Several *familias de la guitarra* have built guitars here for generations, and I have a modest collection of these instruments here on the wall.'

'Two things before you play them…"

"Yes…"

"I do not expect you to decide on a guitar here or now and if you do not ultimately purchase a guitar from me, it is still a rare opportunity for me to share my instruments with someone who can truly appreciate them. I have my musical instrument business and I have my passion for fine instruments. There is some crossover, but as you can see, I keep my interests in different rooms.'

'I am happy to help you find the right guitar for

you, and you are more than welcome to come back and play any guitar you find yourself developing an appreciation for."

"Thank you, Juan. I appreciate the help and generosity…and the other thing?"

"There are many beautiful women in this room who might seduce you with their looks. The eyes are as quick to betray the ears as the heart. May I suggest you wear this blindfold so you might judge them entirely by their voices? Many times, I have people who, once they cannot see, choose instruments with the very attributes they claim to dislike. It is always a surprise to them, but it can be very educating to the ears.'

'I may even throw a few tricks at you."

Tino donned the blindfold, leaned back on his stool and extended his arms. "*Estoy listo.* I am ready."

Antonio took the wheel while Hanns sat beside him with a handheld camera, shooting him in profile. The Spanish countryside rolled by in waves of muted greens and beiges.

"You must be hating this," joked Tino from the back seat where he sat with Veronica.

"Why do you say that?"

"I didn't think you would trust anyone else to drive, but I don't think you trust anyone else to hold the camera either."

"Guilty as charged," Hanns smiled back. "Be glad there's only one of me."

"So, Antonio, we are headed off to the *Ganaderia de Miura* bull ranch. Tell us a bit about Spanish fighting bulls."

"In the *corrida*—the bullfight, the bull is a very important part of the performance. You may have a very good *matador* but if the bull is not brave or fierce, if he is unwilling to charge, if he is clumsy or slow or stupid, it is, for the crowd, a disappointment. The bull must be able to challenge the *matador*, to learn quickly and to present a risk. The *aficionados* do not pay to watch a man in a fancy suit stand in a field with a farm animal.'

'Just as animals may be bred for their meat or milk-producing ability, bulls in *España* have been bred for intelligence, size, speed and ferocity over many generations, and there are several *líneas de sangre*—lines of blood—from which are known the best bulls.'

'Part of the *corrida* is simple showmanship; some bulls are bred to put on a graceful show like those from the *familia* of Domecq. Domecq bulls are popular with the crowd—almost like dancing bulls—but the bulls with the most *bravura* are the *toros de* Miura. Domecq bulls are quite dangerous, but Miura bulls are bigger, meaner and smarter. A Miura is the real test for a *matador*, and many *matador*es have been killed and injured by Miuras. Manolete, one of the greatest *toreros* ever, was killed by a Miura bull in 1947."

"So how do they train these animals?"

"*Actualmente*, they are very careful *not* to train the bulls. When the bull is ready for the *corrida* at four or five years old, it is best he has never seen how the *corrida* works. The bulls live in a field together and learn from each other. Sometimes they fight, but mostly, they happily run free, grazing on wild asparagus and grass. The bull who enters the ring is a wild animal, but he is a *smart* wild animal.

Each bull is observed from the time he is a calf. How does he behave? Is he dominant? Is he easily scared? Does he grow to be large? The *familia* Miura has been raising fighting bulls since 1842. Only the best bulls are used for breeding, and with each generation, the Miura bulls grow bigger, stronger and more dangerous. A Miura bull costs two times the price of another fighting bull. He wants only one thing—to kill the *matador*."

"The cows are also quite fierce, and they are bred for this. They do not go to the *corrida*, but they are used for training and observed for how they react to the *matador* and the *muleta*—the cape. And *mi amigo*, a Miura cow is not as big as a Miura bull, but she is still *muy peligroso*—very dangerous. Only the smartest and most aggressive cows are used to continue the *línea*. The cows' horns are smaller, but cows are tested without *pics*, or *banderillas*, so they are less likely to keep their heads low. I will show you today."

The Andalusian countryside rolled by, dry and sparsely-treed. Signs in the fields—dark silhouettes of gigantic Spanish bulls—loomed over the landscape.

"Stop here for a moment?" said Hanns.

He opened up the sunroof, and stood on the

armrests of the two front seats, pulling his camera up after him and placing it on his shoulder.

"Now, drive in slowly, but cross from the left side of the road to the right as you enter the gate.

Antonio reached behind Hanns's left foot, shifted the Citröen into first gear and rolled smoothly down the dirt road as Hanns had instructed. Hanns angled his camera upwards as they passed through the entrance; a gate consisting of two vertical posts with another nailed across the tops to form a primitive arch. Wooden letters reading "MIURA" had been fashioned from small, straight logs, and on either side of the letters, a sun-bleached bull's skull stared across the land.

As planned, the sun passed behind the letters as they drove beneath them, highlighting them dramatically. Hanns smiled, replaying the shot in his mind.

The Citröen continued down the dirt farm road between fenced pastures dotted with oak trees and grazing bulls with coats of black, white, gray, brown and dappled blends.

Hanns returned to his seat, aiming the camera back at Antonio.

"Like many other animals, these *toros* are raised to be killed and eaten, but they are never crowded together or treated poorly before that happens. In these pastures, the bulls are fed the best food and looked after by a veterinarian. You will not find another domestic animal cared for so well."

"I don't object to how they live," said Veronica from the back seat. "My problem is with how they die."

"You imagine animals at a slaughter house die quickly and painlessly, but this is not always the case. Killing is a bad business and people who do it all day—whether they are killing animals or killing people on a battle field—become tragically insensitive to suffering and death. Have you ever killed anything, Veronica?"

"No."

"…But you are eating a chicken sandwich. Would you eat chicken if you had to raise it and then chop off its head or break its neck?'

'We live in a time and place where we can buy bloodless meat in nice, clean packages covered with plastic and cut into slices that look nothing like an animal part. We do not have to confront the violence or look the animal in the eye, hear it scream or see it tremble with fear. Do you really think your steak dinner or your chicken sandwich died with a smile on its face?'

'The *torero* is criticized for killing the bull, but at least he has the courage to look the bull in the eye and confront death—both the bull's and his own. It is a sad thing when any person becomes numb to killing—when he loses his *compasión*—and can no longer feel a sense of loss over the death of another. Life is a profound mystery and ending another life is no less *profundo*. There is a natural business of predators and prey, of hunting and eating, of defending ourselves and our *familias*. To survive, we must see our prey, our victim, our enemy as an object—maybe even as deserving to die.'

'In this respect, I am maybe no longer a "virgin." When I first began to study *toreo*, I was scared to finish the bull. I liked the dance with the bull, but did not like to kill. The other *estudiantes* laughed at me. They wanted to show they were tougher than the bull, to beat the bull…to kill the bull. But my teacher was a *matador* who had fought many, many *corridas*. He told me, 'Antonio, this is a dance of death. If you want to be a *torero*, you must not hesitate. If you have doubt or regret, you will not survive in *la corrida*', but he also told the others, "the dance of death is also a dance of life. The bull wants to kill you as much as you want to kill him, and he also wants to live as much as you want to live. The moment of killing is only the end of the bull-fight. It is a destination, but *aficionados* come to see *matadores* who give them a good journey. If you are here only to kill, you may convince yourself you are man enough to defeat a big animal with a sword and a cape, and then leave with your stories and your ignorance—and that only if you are extremely lucky."'

'I will always remember the face of the first bull I killed. He was brown like chocolate and looked at me sadly. I have only been in a *corrida* with a few bulls, so I have not experienced many others, but I could see the intelligence in this one. He was smart enough to know he had moved me. He made me hesitate, and I was very fortunate he did not injure me when he threw me in the air and tried to gore me. It did not matter we connected as living beings. He was big, smart, mean, and bred to kill *matador*es. I got up and faced him and killed my bull."

"How did that make you feel?" asked Hanns.

"I wanted to feel sad for ending the life of the bull, but I did not. I felt a powerful excitement, a sense of victory...something else I cannot quite describe. I felt *alive*. Maybe in some way, I felt sad that I did not feel sad. I thought that feeling strong—that I had won— was maybe a primitive thing. I wanted to feel I still had my *compasión*, my innocence. I had spilled the blood of an intelligent creature; one I had made an intelligent connection with. In my head, I wanted to regret killing him but in my heart, I did not. My desire from that point was not to kill more bulls, but I did want to *face* more bulls—to experience again the dance of life and death.'

'Veronica, do you think less of me, your brother who can kill without *compasión*? Before you answer me, consider whether it is any better to buy meat from the *carnicería* that has been killed and prepared for you. Maybe this allows you to keep your *compasión*, but the outcome for the animal is the same. The *qualidad* of its life is far worse. The method of its death and the extent of its suffering is unknown. Standing on top of a hill of things you do not know and cannot see, it may be easy to imagine you look down on other people, but we both kill for our food and ignorance is a poor shield for something as delicate as innocence."

"But Antonio…"

"Let me finish and then I will hear you.'

'I hope you never find yourself having to kill anything, for yes, you will lose something beautiful on that day, and you will always know from that time on you have the ability to take a life…but do not imagine you have nothing to do with the violence of death or with causing that violence to happen. The plastic wrap on your meat may *look* transparent, but few can see through it. Do you really believe you have any less blood on your hands than I have on mine?"

Veronica looked indignant. "But I do not seek out animals and kill them in front of others for entertainment. I do not kill animals as part of some sort of sadistic contest. You are right. I am afraid to look the animal in the eye and take its life, but if I had to take its life, it would happen as quickly and painlessly as possible and only because I needed to eat.'

"What do you think, Hanns?" asked Veronica, as much out of interest in his response as in shifting the focus away from herself.

"I'm not sure you'll care for my answer. I did some hunting and spent some time on a farm as a child and became acquainted with killing and preparing meat at a young age. I imagine I went through some of the same poetic questioning Antonio just shared with us, but that kind of thinking is more abstract when you are a child. In my world, I saw chickens beheaded. I saw the throats of pigs cut. These were all animals I cared for and knew personally, but when they ended up on my dinner plate, I quickly acclimated to the idea that this was their place in life. I was always thankful to them, and definitely acknowledged they had given something to me, but I grew up with the idea that domestic animals had domestic purposes; even animals I knew by name.'

'I see both sides, but I don't find myself feeling very sentimental for the bull. He's basically a big, nasty creature descended from a long line of big, nasty creatures. As a domestic animal, his place in the world is ordained by man—not by God and not by himself. He'll live *la vida buena* for four or five years and then he'll be sent to the *corrida* where his chances of survival are slim, yet infinitely better than that of your average beef steer. He will experience pain and fear and probably death, and this is regrettable…but how many animals or even people really have the luxury of peacefully growing old and passing calmly away in their sleep? How many people or animals live a life so free from pain or the need to fight for survival? The bull may have a hard time of it during his final fifteen minutes, but we should all pray to live so well and die so easily.'

'My perspective is a practical one. We could put an end to *toreo* and put an end to the breeding of Spanish bulls and do you think we would have any impact at all on the amount of suffering in the world? We all suffer. We all struggle to survive and then we all die. Hopefully, we get to experience a little joy and pleasure along the way. The Spanish bull certainly gets his share and as far as I'm concerned, this puts him among nature's elite. You won't catch me in the ring with him, but any concerns I might have about the circumstances of his demise are outweighed by my admiration for the quality of his life. He is a simple creature who requires far less than we people do to be happy. He does not philosophize or intellectualize about his existence and asks only for food, water and the company of his kind. He receives all of this and more from the day of his birth through the day of his death. When I look at the larger picture, I find little to protest."

"And you know," interrupted Antonio "that a sloppy kill is the mark of a poor *matador*. The crowd wants to see the *matador* win, but they do not wish the bull to suffer. When the bull falls and can no longer fight, he is immediately killed with a dagger to the spine just behind the head. This kills him like a lightning bolt. *Compasión* does have a place in the *corrida*."

Antonio turned off the engine in front of a low, whitewashed building with painted yellow accents, and the group clambered out into the Spanish sunshine and stretched.

"You're awfully quiet, Tino," said Hanns, pointing his camera. "What's going on in that artist's brain?"

"Since you're asking…I stopped eating meat when I

married my wife. It was her conviction that because we are fortunate to live in a land where we have easy access to fresh fruits, vegetables and grains, it is not necessary for us to kill either directly or indirectly to survive. I have been eating this way for many years now, and I'm healthy and happy. On the very few occasions I've eaten meat since then, it didn't sit well in my stomach and I've lost any craving for it or interest in it.

I lean towards agreeing with my wife, but not everyone has our same circumstances. It's fine for people who live near the ocean to eat fish. People who live in the woods can eat wild game and people who live on the prairie can eat cute little bunny rabbits. Questions about ethical violence only arise among people who have the rare luxury to exercise some choice in the matter. The relationship between man and animals is tied to the relationship between man and his larger environment. When the environment gives you choices, you can deliberate. If the environment gives you only seafood, you're better off shutting up and eating your fish.'

'As a child, I also witnessed and participated in the killing of animals for food. Today, I have a difficult time imagining myself killing anything, but that probably has to do with my lack of interest.'

'Should we kill when we don't have to? For me,

the answer is no, but that's not my prescription for the world. A lot of unhappy people believe we should apply the same guidelines to our personal lives and engage in sex only for the purpose of having children. Ethics and practicality are strange bedfellows; if we equate "good" with "necessary," the world gets pretty boring pretty quickly'

'If you don't like violence, don't engage in it and don't cause it indirectly; don't eat animals at all— I don't—but I don't care if anyone else does. As I said earlier, debating the matter is a luxury most people on planet Earth can't afford, and..." Tino looked at Veronica. "don't believe you're incapable of violence, yourself.'

'You may think nothing of killing a cockroach or slapping a mosquito. If you are sufficiently hungry or sufficiently threatened, you will think as little of strangling a man with your bare hands or killing a bull with a sword.'

'There is a bull inside each of us. We may live out our lives peacefully with the bull sleeping quiet and happy and forgotten. Those of us who sing, play an instrument, paint, make love, or climb mountains may not even know when we are riding on his back, but if circumstances warrant it, the horns come out, the bull snorts, paws the earth and charges. He is unquestionably bigger and stronger than the *matador*.'

'The whole matter is ultimately something of an elitist conversation. Like rich people debating the merits of an economic policy while at the same time they're oblivious to the plight of a starving child in a faraway land, it's a "small picture" conversation. You can stab the bull with a sword and make his body die, but if you could really kill him once-and-for-all, would there be any need to fight him over and over?'

'Kill the bull? Spare the bull? It makes no difference. *Toreo* is an art that has powerful meaning to some people, little significance to others, and absolutely zero practical value whatsoever to anyone. Trying to understand art is like trying to understand God. If you can handle either of those two, try understanding *man*.

If you like it, it's art, if you don't like it, it's *mierda*. Everyone's a critic...but the artist, like the bull, can never truly be killed. Ascribing rightness or wrongness to art, bullfighting or killing in general is naive."

"There will be no killing today," said Antonio, "so regardless of how any of you may feel about *toreo*, I invite all of you to come and see the strength and beauty of the most ferocious creatures in Spain."

"Will you be picking an opponent…or a partner here at the ranch?" asked Veronica, trying to be civil.

"The *matador* does not have that luxury. I just wanted to take a look and give Hanns a chance to learn about the *toros* and shoot some film. I am to participate in a *corrida* a week from Friday in *Ronda*. The bulls will be Miuras from right here, but we won't know which ones until just before the *corrida*. At that time, each of the three *matadores* will draw lots to choose two bulls each.'

'Let me go tell *Señor* Miura we are here, and I will show you the bulls up close. If I can, I will try to work with some of the cows so you can film some of the passes."

Inside the compound, Hanns aimed his camera at a huge white bull standing alone in a corral. The animal stood in profile, aloof, powerful and proud. It stared at him and snorted disinterestedly with ribbons of mucous streaming from its nostrils. The bull put on no noticeable display of aggression, and it was easy to imagine that had the animal already gotten the whole story of the *corrida* from a pardoned friend, the matter was of no great concern to him.

"Kill me?" chuckled the bull. "Kill me? Feel free to try. Let's dance."

"Anna, How was your flight?" asked Hanns. "I hope you didn't suffer too much with the airline food."

"I worried when Andreas started requesting aerobatic maneuvers, but our Captain managed to keep him satisfied with just one roll. Frankly, it was more terrifying to anticipate it than to actually experience it. With regard to the food, your friend Kalimba here is quite the gourmet. In the absence of high-G turns and weightless falls, I was able to both enjoy the food and keep it down."

Andreas spread his arms and made an airplane sound with a big grin. Kalimba patted him on the head affectionately, and Anna smiled warmly at both of them.

"Welcome to *Sevilla*," said Hanns.

"Thanks for sending for us. I felt as if this magical whirlwind of adventure had spontaneously sprung up in my living room and then just-as-suddenly blown away through the window along with its cast of unusual characters. I'm very glad to see the Gods have seen fit to keep me on the stage, and in the absence of a script, I will do my best to improvise something eloquent, entertaining and meaningful.'

'How is my Tino?"

"How is Tino? In some ways, good, because a fine guitar dealer has befriended him and out of genuine affection or hope for commercial gain…or possibly both…has been bringing over a different guitar each day for him to play. And I think, for the same reason, he is frustrated. The wide selection has broadened his palette somewhat, but he hasn't found an instrument that appeals to him in the same way as his old *guitarra*. When you reject the World's finest because you know there's something better out there, you inevitably begin to question whether your own tastes are based on reality or delusion. It's a good thing he's a master player because he's rejected some expensive and highly desirable instruments, some of which were once owned by flamenco legends. If he couldn't play, he'd have been laughed out of *Sevilla* as a philistine with a tin ear.'

'But he's been practicing in his room—which keeps him sane, and at night, he plays at the flamenco bars where he's been a huge hit with both the audience and the dancers. He's been teaching us all to count *compás*.'

'All-in-all, you'll find we've been taking pretty good care of him in your absence, but I'm looking forward to seeing his face when he sees you. It'll add some fuel to his fire to have you in the audience tonight"

"Audience?"

"Nothing big or formal—just a small gathering of players and listeners."

"I'll look forward to that," smiled Anna.

"And how about you Kalimba? I'm impressed you were able to show such restraint given the plane I hooked you up with. I had to call in quite a few old favors to get a bird like that."

"My dear Hanns, while you are filming the slaughter in tomorrow afternoon's *corrida*, if you have any questions about my whereabouts, you need only look up, squint your eyes and look for the tiny speck in the sky that will be me exploring the outermost limits of your flying Ferrari. Access to a machine like that is a rare opportunity I can assure you will not be wasted."

"Let's get the bags stowed and go surprise Tino. I asked him to wait for us for dinner, but he doesn't know you're coming. We'll have a nice, long, traditional Spanish meal as nothing much happens in *Sevilla* before 11:00 at night. Antonio's sister, Veronica, is willing to watch Andreas tonight and he'll be fast asleep before he even knows he's with a baby sitter. We'll head over the bridge to *Triana* where the tourists don't usually go, and listen to Tino join the local musical melee.'

'Flamenco is often presented as high Spanish culture. Some practice and perform it admirably as a classical art and there are many imitators, but real flamenco comes from the street. It's secular music; a musical lamentation of the poor and downtrodden rooted more in the ancient traditions of gypsies than in the halls of academia or studios of modern dance. You can polish flamenco, but if you overdo it, you just grind away the grit of life that makes it flamenco in the first place.'

'At this particular period in time, many Spanish gypsies are being relocated by the Franco government from their traditional gypsy quarter in *Triana* to the *Las Tres Mil Viviendas barrio* at the south end of town. It's unfortunate for the gypsies, but perhaps it fuels the fires of suffering that make for great flamenco music?"

"What really is it about gypsies that makes everyone despise them so?" asked Anna. "Hitler exterminated thousands of them, and everyone's always shuttling them here and there, moving them out of the way."

"Let me field this one," offered Kalimba. "The Roma people have distinguishing racial features, and I can tell you from personal experience this makes people naturally uncomfortable. It leads to segregated— often self-segregated—societies, which is what leads to different races developing different cultures, which brings about more segregation, separation and alienation."

"Who am I, but a white-skinned, blue-eyed, blonde-haired German who, by physical appearance, would have been a poster-boy for the Hitler youth, to contradict you?" interjected Hanns, "but I don't think I'm being racist when I warn you to keep your hands on your money when you see gypsies in the street. My understanding is that kleptomania is academic to gypsy culture. Gypsies aren't taught that stealing is wrong. They're taught as children to be expert thieves and to regard anyone who isn't a gypsy as a potential target. That smacks of its own kind of racism to me."

"And it may be true to a greater or lesser extent," returned Kalimba. "I've heard the same things, but I don't personally know any gypsies. If it is the case, I think it's better we object to that aspect of the culture than to the race itself. I'm willing to bet people can't be genetically predisposed towards kleptomania. I'm also inclined to believe there are more and less honorable gypsies and probably, it's the dishonest ones who show up on the social radar."

"I'm all for extending the benefit of the doubt," said Hanns. "I can't argue that the white man has any kind of historical record for integrity; we're probably the worst offenders of all, but we're less known for petty theft than for grand fraud. One of the most successful of those frauds was arranging to have that larger kind of crime show up on an entirely separate radar screen from the one pickpockets and muggers show up on, but I have personally had to scare the crap out of a few gypsy kids who tried to slip their fingers into my pocket. I have reliable sources who tell me gypsy camps are littered with garbage and human shit. I never made a comment about gypsies as a race, but as a culture, their disregard for hygiene and personal property is not likely to endear them to any post-medieval society."

"Victimhood is an ages-old survival technique," said Anna, "and however unfortunate their lot may be, I have to wonder if not competing for power and land isn't a good way to play safe?'

'Even stationary gypsies seem to maintain a certain nomadic character. They may live for years in a tent or shack that has an entirely temporary quality to it, never adding amenities like plumbing or running water that would connect it to the grid and give it any air of permanence or grounding. Even if they're not traveling, they don't seem to be much concerned about owning and accumulating land. As such, they're decidedly different from the various other Western cultures they live among, all of which place great value on the questionable concept of private land-ownership. American Indians saw things this way; the land was theirs to wander over and derive a livelihood from, but the idea of one man or even one tribe actually claiming ownership of it made no sense to them.'

'But the creative output of the gypsies suggests it's impossible to dismiss them as belonging to any kind of lesser culture. Flamenco singing, dancing and guitar are all highly-developed art forms contributed by the gypsies that Spain claims as her own…and I wonder how our friend Antonio would handle the suggestion that gypsies contributed to the development of *toreo*."

Kalimba waved himself into the conversation. "The great Django Reinhardt was a Belgian gypsy guitarist who lived in a caravan with his clan. He originally played banjo in the French musette bands and later took up the guitar. After hearing Louis Armstrong, he developed the first original European jazz style and eventually toured the States with Duke Ellington. Gypsy jazz has *aficionados* all over the planet, but has its roots in the same Romani culture that flamenco does. Though the French often claim Django's style as their own, in these days of cassette tapes and radio, gypsy swing music is infinitely more accessible to people who live on the road than at any previous time in history, and is much less likely to be stolen from its true inventors. Django recorded hundreds of tracks. I understand many modern gypsies own these recordings and take pride in this music as their own sophisticated contribution to modern global culture.'

'In Spain, gypsies play flamenco, but elsewhere, they play hot swing around the campfire. Flamenco, gypsy swing, and also bebop and blues do much to oppose any notion that race, education, social status or economic standing impairs any people's ability to create important new languages for the global dialog."

"I wouldn't argue against any of it," said Hanns. "By all means, let's remain open-minded in *Triana* tonight, but let's not sacrifice our wallets to the gods of idealism, either. There may be honor among thieves, and there may be no thieves at all, but I have no need to prove it one way or the other by being vulnerable. You won't find me turning down any opportunities to let real circumstances inform my prejudices, but I'll risk sounding closed-minded if it offers us a modicum of safety."

Hanns carried Anna's bags across the parking lot towards the Citröen parked adjacent to the door of a building on the opposite side. A tow-truck had parked directly behind it and a character in blue coveralls was just starting to operate the levers on his hydraulic towing apparatus.

"Hey! *Amigo! Alto!* Stop! *Es mi coche*—my car," shouted Hanns, quickening his walk towards the vehicle but not quite able to break into a run because of the suitcases he was carrying.

The truck operator was unmoved, and almost imperceptibly shrugged his shoulders.

Kalimba arrived first and began conversing with the tow-truck man in Spanish, his eloquence and presence in combination with his dark skin and long dreadlocks commanding the man's interest and attention.

After a short exchange during which Kalimba spoke slowly and calmly and, as far as Hanns could tell, entirely without a trace of accent, he stopped and translated. "Apparently, this parking space is a loading zone until after 5:00 P.M."

"But it's 5:30 now," protested Hanns, "and we can't have been parked here more than 20 minutes."

Hanns, red-faced and clench-fisted, glared at the tow-truck operator who responded with arrogant disinterest.

Kalimba put a hand on Hanns's shoulder.

After another brief exchange with the tow man, Kalimba withdrew his billfold, handed the man some money and with a nod, he simply got back into his truck and drove away.

"My friend," said Kalimba, "you are preoccupied with being *right*. You don't really believe the laws of the land here offer you genuine protection, do you? Laws, either legal or spiritual, depend on the same source of fiction for their value as the notion that there are true sources of authority to issue them. In any case, the organizations that sanction these artificial laws and values are historically well-known to operate primarily out of self-interest.'

'As a foreigner, the legal system here would not place your rights above those of a Spaniard. It is in the government's interest to cultivate the loyalty of its own subjects—and they have no reason to give a shit about you one way or the other. Is it wrong? Sure. Is it morally reprehensible? Of course…but in the grand scheme of things, if you can't pay, you can't play.'

'Spain is governed by *Señor* Franco's World War II-style dictatorship that has little regard for its own subjects' ideals about rights and freedom, never mind yours or mine. People who make trouble here get *disappeared*."

"I suppose you're right," said Hanns reflecting on Kalimba's words.

Kalimba laughed. "You're just used to winning. You have expectations that the game works a certain way like it does at home. You understand how to work that system and how to circumvent it when you need to. Here, there is no winning—at least on the surface level. If you win, you lose. If you lose, you win—at least in the eyes of a government that only feels safe when the people are losing.

'Here, things happen underground. Commerce happens on the black market. The black market is run by the Spanish mafia, and in a country like this, organized crime can only function because it's in bed with the government. Because the government is working both sides of the street, it also protects people. It's in the Government's best interest to look the other way as long as nobody is muscling in on their business. On some levels, it's not much different than capitalism or any other type of competitive food chain. People want food, shelter and security, and if these basic needs are threatened, social values melt away like butter; people focus on taking care of themselves.'

'The tow truck operator saw your foreign plates and probably just waited for us to come back out and pay him off. He can feed his family and buy his smokes without worrying about accidentally towing the car of someone connected with the regime. You're a safe target because he's higher on the political food chain than you. Tough luck."

"Kalimba, I'm enjoying your explanation, and I think it's important for me to remind myself that stupidity can happen with tremendous efficiency here. It won't help me to be overconfident…but…and this may seem strange to you…what I'm really curious about is the name of the towing company. I'll certainly take your sage advice about the politics here."

"These guys are the biggest towing company in Southern Spain. They sprang up about two years ago and now they're everywhere from here to the French border; probably one of those mafia rackets I was just talking about. It's basically legalized auto theft, and it's big money. Ironic for them to call their operation *'Hombre Honesto'* isn't it?"

Hanns began to laugh, slowly at first and then tears streamed down his face. He crossed his arms, leaned against the Citröen and could hardly breathe. Anna put a hand on his shoulder to make sure he was okay, and he was only able to gasp something about "not pee in my pants." Kalimba wondered what the joke was and young Andreas began to laugh at Hanns's laughing.

"So someone who had been out of the country for a few years might not know this company?" croaked Hanns after he had composed himself slightly.

"Probably not," replied Kalimba, "but I'm guessing there's more to the joke than getting ripped off by the 'honest man?'"

"Ah…they do say no good deed goes unpunished," mused Hanns. "Sorry to leave you wondering, but this is one of those jokes that will lose a lot in translation. Let me keep my story in the bottle until it's had time to ferment. I promise to share the wine with you at some future time. In the interim, would you do me the favor of not mentioning this to Antonio, and especially to Tino? I'm not sure they'd find it quite so funny as I do."

"Do we have a choice?" asked Anna with a shrug.

"I'm guessing we don't," said Kalimba, "but having Hanns owe you a story is never a bad thing. He's a wonderful story-teller and I'm willing to wait."

"So let's be off, then," suggested Anna, giving up hopes of resolving the mystery.

The Citröen zoomed off, back towards the *Calle Adriano*.

Spanish ephemera covered the walls. Bullfighting posters, old flamenco record album covers, the mounted head of a Miura bull and numerous yellowed black and white photographs in cheap frames signed by famous *flamencos* and *toreros* crowded still more frames containing paintings of Moorish castles and Andalusian landscapes. A moustachioed old man sat next to Tino staring powerfully and intently through the audience at something only he could see, clapping perfect and spirited *compás*. Next to him, a slight, black-haired young man with round glasses channeled the spirit of a lamenting voice clearly not of his own body. A wiry dancer floated inside the circle of dark wooden chairs, an arm thrust heavenward, more and more of her hair escaping the prison of a bright red scarf to gyrate wildly about her as she spun, never quite seeming to touch the ground.

A final cry of sorrow from the bespectacled vocalist punctuated the end of the *cante* as the players and the dancer climaxed together. After a stunned silence, the room broke into applause.

Anna kissed Tino on the cheek. "My dear, it

is so wonderful to hear you in this setting instead of alone in your studio or at one of those silly concerts they put you up to back home. You are truly in your element here, and we shouldn't let too much time pass between future trips to Andalusia. You should be doing more of this. I have always seen your brilliant colors, but this is the canvas for which they are intended. It is truly wonderful to discover something new and beautiful about someone I already love so dearly, but…"

"You are tired, *mi amor?*"

"Antonio has offered to drive us back, but you, Kalimba and Hanns can stay as long as you like and take a taxi home. I've had a long day, but I don't want to ruin the party."

Vanessa stood behind Anna with Antonio, looking slightly irritated at the prospect of having a third person along in the vehicle. Antonio smiled warmly, having been carried by Tino's music to a place that to Vanessa's disappointment, betrayed no obvious desire to explore the world beneath her mini-skirt.

Hanns read the script of the upcoming drama on the faces of Antonio and Vanessa intuitively, and whispered a suggestion in Tino's ear that they might do better to stay in *Triana* and avoid the battle. Anna delivered a wink to Hanns communicating that she understood the situation and was more than capable of handling it. The trio exited through the arched doorway and headed off into the night.

Tino turned around to see a thickly-built man wearing a worn military jacket inspecting his guitar. *"Cuidado, amigo. Este guitarra no es…"*

"A very nice instrument. Put it in its case and come with me. You are invited to meet *El Dedo Meñique*… I will not accept a refusal."

Tino looked at Hanns and then at the man making the strange and rather undiplomatic request.

"If it was your guitar I was after, it would already have disappeared," the man declared. "If it was money, there are many small, dark streets here and many people on them less able to defend themselves than you.'

'I am Bernard. Come with me. It is rare to hear a real *flamenco,* and you have earned your invitation. Very few outsiders do. Come quickly."

Bernard walked a few paces ahead of Tino, Kalimba and Hanns, briskly and wordlessly leading them down cobblestoned streets, over fences and across vacant lots where old buildings had been cleared between standing ones. Tino looked at Hanns and shrugged, committed at this point to finding out what lay ahead.

At the end of an alley, they came to a dead end at

a wooden fence. Bernard grabbed two planks near the bottom and swung them outwards from where nails at their tops served as pivots, revealing a low, triangular entrance through which the sounds of laughter and music could be heard.

Bernard looked around and gestured for his guests to follow him inside. "Forgive my terse introduction. Spain is not always friendly to gypsies, and flamenco has become sufficiently popular as a Spanish National art form that some among its *aficionados* resent its gypsy origins. I thought it best to bring you away quickly before anyone noticed you were being stolen…and you may have noticed I did not exactly take the most direct route here?"

Tino shrugged again, but Hanns prided himself in having a fairly accurate natural compass. Though he dismissed the circuitous route as a paranoid expression, he had quietly tucked pieces of shredded cocktail napkin in pay phones, window boxes, and other fortuitous gaps that presented themselves along the way should any necessity of finding their own way home present itself. "I am Hanns," he nodded to his host. "This is Kalimba, and it appears you already know Tino."

A small compound that looked to have once been a freight yard of some sort lay before them. Roofless, doorless and windowless, a one-story building crumbled in the far corner, its openings scorched by some long-ago fire and its walls covered with layers of graffiti. A cluster of rusting shipping containers squatted next to it and, an engineless truck overgrown with weeds perched tireless on stacks of concrete blocks. Wooden shanties sprawled across the cracked concrete floor, connected by clotheslines streaming colorful garments appearing as a sonata in gray under the *Sevillan* moonlight. A scattered collection of motor homes ranging in quality from decrepit hulks to able road-explorers mingled with a smattering of tarps and tents to complete the camp, while the orange flicker of a bonfire in an old barrel revealed silhouettes of dark figures seated around it— their voices, laughter and the tinkling of guitar strings carried like the scent of spice on a warm wind.

"Stay close to me until we are recognized," warned Bernard. He led them first to the truck, then to a dark lamp post standing starkly at the middle of the yard, to another car wreck and then finally towards the fire. "There are two or three paths a gypsy will take to enter here, the straight and direct one silently communicating the greatest danger. We have had no problems for several months now…which is a good thing, but also makes me feel we are overdue for some harassment."

"So, how many are living here?" asked Hanns.

"Nobody *lives* here," returned Bernard. "There are about thirty or forty who *stay* here, but one day, and ideally according to our own plan rather than the *guardia's*, this camp will be left behind overnight, its people carrying with them what they can and abandoning or burning what they can't. To an outsider, it is only a camp, a *barrio*, a small ghetto, and while some real poverty can certainly be found here, the simple homes are as much an expression of impermanence as of their builders' limited means. A few gypsies have found their fortunes, but these are as likely to live in a tent as in one of the motor homes you see parked here."

"And what about sanitation?" asked Kalimba.

"The *Triana* district is almost an island, nestled between two branches of the *Guadalquivir* River; we are right on the water here. An outhouse on the old dock behind the back fence keeps this camp a bit more sanitary than others you may have heard about."

"And pardon me for asking, but Bernard is not exactly a common gypsy name," noted Hanns. "I assume there's a story here?"

Bernard laughed. "I'm an American from New York, and was in the Navy ready to ship out to Vietnam. After a few friends came home in body bags, I got disillusioned. I split for Europe during my final leave before anyone had time to get concerned about my absence.'

'My grandparents were German Jews, young artists who saw the writing on the wall and came to the U.S. with my young father during the early thirties when the Nazis first started heating things up and shutting down the progressive art and architecture schools. A lot of German was spoken in our home, and I had a few other family members who survived the war in Switzerland. We lost a few people, but were one of the luckier families who got out in time.'

'This meant that years later, I had relatives to stay with, and I could speak the language. I settled in, but couldn't officially work in Europe so I started odd-jobbing my way around; traveling as I could with a thumb and a backpack.'

'When I hit Spain, I fell in love with flamenco. It struck me like a fever, and I began to listen and study. My relatives thought I was crazy, but I got deeper and deeper into it. As I became aware of the differences between *tourist* flamenco and *real* flamenco, I began to seek out the hidden clubs and secret gatherings of the true *aficionados*. They're actually all part of a pretty small circle, and before long, I was exchanging familiar nods with the same faces almost every night. There, I had a chance to learn more about the gypsies and when they realized I was serious and without any real place to stay, they took me in.'

'As far as my studies, I can play *palmas* and clap fairly good *compás* but I'm not a natural musician. All the same, the gypsies respect my ear for picking out authentic players who have the *toque* and for what it's worth, I'm slowly working on a book about the gypsies and their music that I get to live and research from the inside. It sure beats the hell out of humping an M-16 through the jungles of Southeast Asia.'

'Flamenco happens in the nightclubs, but flamenco also happens here in the streets where the voices of poverty and the good, hard, simple life blend together in joyful lament. When I heard you play, Tino, I wanted to bring you and this side of the music together. Also, if I'm not mistaken, I think I see gypsy blood in your features, and I'm curious to see how your roots will react to their native soil.'

'Come; let's play some music while there is still some night left."

Bernard led his guests quietly towards the fire and motioned towards some empty folding chairs. Two men played guitars and another sat with eyes closed atop a battered *cajón*—a percussion box over which his hands moved deftly and precisely. The voices of the two guitars weaved in and around each other, and as the fire light flared up, one of the players—clearly the more proficient of the two—was revealed to be an expressionless boy of about twelve whose small hands danced over the strings.

"El Dedo Meñique," whispered Bernard. "They call him 'the little finger.' He has been playing in the gypsy camps since he was four. He does not read or write or go to school. He hardly talks…but when he is not sleeping, he is playing the guitar. Some accomplished players think he has made a deal with the devil—or that he actually *is* the devil, and there has been trouble—so the gypsies just keep him to themselves as a sort of private treasure. He is happy to stay with his family and tribe where he has the freedom to play all the time.'

'Things are casual and easy here, Tino. Go ahead. Take your guitar. Play with *El Dedo Meñique*. See what happens."

Tino took a deep breath, stretched his hands and cracked his knuckles before quietly flipping open the latches of the guitar case. Almost inaudibly, he tuned his instrument, taking care to integrate the sound of the tuning rhythmically and melodically into the music, and then after another short pause to listen, he closed his eyes and began to play.

A smile slowly appeared on the boy's face as he sensed Tino's ability and presence. He offered a phrase to Tino who immediately improvised a musical response. *El Dedo* answered and then, anticipating Tino's phrase, followed with a perfect harmony line beneath it. The second guitarist stopped playing so he could listen. The fire crackled as something collapsed inside the barrel and a torrent of sparks flew up into the darkness. Tino and the boy chased each other, alternately testing each other and providing musical support for one another's melodic excursions, exploring the boundaries of technique and time, whispering, shouting, making love, waging war, praying, damning and transporting all who listened to a world beyond matter and energy. The percussionist cried out unconsciously from his trance.

For an eternal hour or more, the two guitarists cavorted. The boy broke a string and kept playing. Almost immediately after, one of Tino's strings gave way but the dance continued. Finally, with a woody twang, another string popped on Tino's guitar and the music collapsed into laughter.

Tino embraced the boy like an old friend, and bowed to him. *"¡Bravo, amigo. Maravilloso!"*

Wordlessly, the boy smiled and gracefully bowed his head in return. Hanns's eyes sparkled in the fire light, and Kalimba leaned back contentedly in his chair; arms crossed and feet propped up on an old milk crate.

While Tino and the boy restrung and retuned, a few more men with guitars came to sit by the fire. Another man tossed some boards into the barrel and the flames climbed high once again, revealing the faces and instruments of the ring of musicians in orange contrast to the blackness of the night. One of the guitarists started a *bulería* and a man appeared out of the shadows to sing an interpretation of a Lorca poem. A dark woman wearing a long white skirt and a simple black tube top began to weave before the orange light as the music rose, the dancing flames revealing the delicate shape of her lithe figure through the cotton gauze. The players shouted back and forth to encourage one another until a nod brought the performance to a perfectly coordinated finish that froze the dancer, her anguished face looking downward and two fingers pressed to her brow as if in mourning.

Tino turned to Hanns with excitement on his face. "Can you hear these instruments? I hear something different here…a familiar voice I have not heard yet in any of the guitars I have played in *Sevilla*."

Hanns motioned apologetically that he was unable to hear the difference. Kalimba continued to recline and smile meditatively, but Bernard saw Tino's wonderment. "I am not a great musician but the gypsies give me credit for having a natural ear. I hear what you are hearing. With the gypsies, beginner guitarists start out on any old instrument they can find or steal. As part of their training, to prove they are serious, they must learn to produce good tone and technique from these tired old boxes. It is thought that real musicianship and authentic flamenco sound comes from the *toque*—not from the instrument itself.'

'There may be some truth in this, but I am not a gypsy myself, and I am not tied to the mythology and tradition as they are. It's a good learning technique if it doesn't put you off on playing altogether, but the truth is I've heard players who started on mediocre instruments make quantum leaps on the day they finally got a good guitar. To some extent, a craftsman can only be as great as his tools are sharp. Nothing sounds as beautiful to me as a great player married to a great instrument.'

'When they are ready, gypsy *tocaores* will buy a guitar from one of only a very few luthiers. As you may know, a really good *guitarra* can be expensive and often requires a few years of waiting while the builder creates instruments for other players ahead of you in line. When a gypsy player begins to show real talent, he is considered to be a sacred carrier of the tradition. If he is willing to dedicate himself to becoming a vessel for the spirit of flamenco, his people will scrape together the funds to purchase a good instrument for him."

One of the men sitting around the fire got up to leave and bumped Bernard as he passed by.

"There is a maker in *Ronda* who builds guitars only for gypsies. He does not put a label in his guitars and I don't know his name—and if you ask the gypsies, you are not likely to get a straight answer. All-the-same, I can't imagine he's really as secret and difficult-to-find as legend makes him out to be. I'll try to do some research for you when the *sangría* is flowing. Then, it will not be difficult to get an exchange of stories started among the *tocaores* about how they found their instruments."

"The only reason I am in Spain is to find an instrument to replace a very special one that was destroyed," explained Tino. "If you can point me in the right direction, I would be very, very grateful."

"Meet me two nights from tonight outside the flamenco club. I'll bring you back here to play some more and try to have an answer for you."

"*Muchas Gracias*, Bernard...and with that, I'm

afraid I see light on the horizon. Unfortunately, we need to be getting back to the people we'll be weighing down with our lack of sleep later today. It's been a marvelous evening, and rarely have I had an opportunity to play with the likes of these musicians." Tino stretched a hand out, placed the other on his heart and bowed his head to the gypsies who now sat smoking quietly around the dwindling fire.

"A fascinating and beautiful experience," declared Hanns. "I have always liked and appreciated flamenco, but am only now beginning to understand why people become so passionate about it. When you strip away the false veneers that are applied to make it sound more 'genuine' to the uneducated listener, something truly spiritual and ethereal and powerful emerges—a feeling I am having difficulty putting into words. The music brought unexpected tears to me. I can't explain it, but I hear a strange sorrow carried in the music that…"

"*Duende*," said Bernard. "A certain feeling. Don't attempt to put your finger on it, or name it, or explain it. *Duende* is the spirit of flamenco and its presence is the only true measure by which one can judge the authenticity of the music. It does not come from an instrument; it does not come from a technique, or even from within the player. It is something more and different, but the closest you will ever get to defining it is to identify what it is *not*. You have experienced it and it is real. What it actually *is* is unimportant."

Kalimba laughed his soft, deep, warm resonant laugh and broke his silence. "Thank you for having us, Bernard. I confess I was concerned at first, but life offers rare occasion to view its more exotic slices from the inside. There is no way to contrive for this to happen. You must be ready and open to those opportunities when they come your way. I am always grateful when fate magically brings me to some place I would never have imagined myself being, and to the company of some of the good and secret people who live in the shadows."

"You are all welcome, my friends, and welcome to visit us again. I'll escort you to where you can get a ride home," replied Bernard.

Four dark figures emerged noiselessly from between the planks of the old fence and headed east over cobblestoned streets towards where the glow of the lights of *Sevilla* mixed sweetly with the dawn.

Smells of fried food and cigar smoke mixed with the sounds of the crowd as they filed into the arena, choosing their places on rings of hard, concrete benches. Some brought cushions with them or purchased them from a booth near the entrance. Many of the locals dressed colorfully for the *corrida;* a few even wore business attire in spite of the afternoon's heat. A range of visitors crowded the stands including a tour-group of overweight Americans, and a smattering of hippies in tattered T-shirts. Dark-haired families, some including three or four generations, chattered away loudly in Spanish.

"We are lucky today," said Antonio. "First, our flat is across the street from *la corrida*—which saves us the hassle and expense of parking. Second, *El Cordobes* is fighting the last *corrida* today; he's a great master *torero* who will soon be retiring. One of his *picadores* is an old friend of mine, so I have arranged for special seats and permission to film from anywhere we like."

Hanns wore a photographer's vest, its pockets stuffed with lenses and other paraphernalia. A note pad extended from his shirt pocket where it was tucked in with a selection of pens, under which was clipped a very official-looking ID badge. His sunglasses hung from a neck-strap, and perched rakishly atop his head was a khaki-colored Panama hat with a yellow band that read:

"PRENSA • PRESS • PRESSE • STAMPA"

Anna shot an impressed eyebrow up at Hanns.

"All home-made, my dear…and completely without any connection to a real news agency or publication, but why let the truth stand in the way of a good story? If it walks like a journalist and quacks like a journalist, it must be a journalist. Nobody has time to bother verifying the credentials of a harmless photographer, especially such an official-looking one, if I don't say so myself…and nobody wants to risk upsetting the person they're hoping to get a good write-up from. This get-up has gotten me into places where anyone else in plain clothes would be stuck in a security queue for days. I climb where no one is allowed to climb, and walk back-stage into the intimate dressing rooms of life's performances."

Anna chuckled over Hanns's confidence in the power of his contrived appearances and held Andreas's hand. Tino followed as they made their way towards the front row, checking their tickets against the faded numbers stenciled on the concrete.

Having placed his cushion on one of the seats, Hanns left Tino and his family to find a vantage point from which to photograph the contest.

The *pasadoble* began to play, and a ceremonious parade of horses and colorfully-dressed *toreros* circled the ring. Anticipation grew as the first *corrida* was announced.

Hanns hovered precariously from an archway over the gate as it opened to release the first bull into the ring. The reddish-brown animal charged valiantly at first, running straight to the center and eyeing the crowd malevolently, but then stood frozen and stupefied. A man emerged from the perimeter and waved a cape at the bull, who took a few steps and then stopped, pawing the earth nervously. The crowd of spectators hissed and booed loudly until some men on horseback and a few steers were sent out to guide the reluctant bovine out of the ring.

"Sometimes," explained Antonio who had taken his seat next to Andreas with Tino and Anna, "you don't get a good bull. Maybe the bull knows what is happening and doesn't want to play?"

A few minutes later, a large black mass hurtled out

of the gate. Hanns photographed the afternoon sunlight glinting against its muscles and filtering through the clouds of dust around its hooves. The enraged animal was clearly unhappy to be in the ring, and was easily provoked to charge by the *cuadrillos* who emerged from different parts of the perimeter to keep it running and confused. The crowd was happier now; this animal clearly showed much more spirit and ferocity.

The bull was made to run for a few minutes before the *matador* came out and let the bull run a few passes. "He is testing the bull," explained Antonio to young Andreas. "He wants to see if the bull hooks to one side when he charges. Do you see how the bull favors the right horn? Watch…"

After a few minutes, the *picadores* came out on horses with their lances. "Why are the horses blindfolded?" asked Andreas.

"The bull has very sharp horns, and you will see him charge at the horses in a moment. Do you see the heavy blankets that cover the horses? They are not for decoration. They protect the horses from the horns of the bull. When the bull charges, the man on the horse will poke him in the neck with his *pic*. The blindfold keeps the horse from seeing the bull and being afraid. It keeps him steady for the *picador*."

"Doesn't the *pic* hurt the bull?" asked Andreas with concern, trying to be heard over the din of the crowd.

"I think for a big bull, the little stick is like a bee sting. It hurts a little bit, but not very much. Right now, the bull thinks he is stronger than anything. If he gets hurt just a little, he will be angry, but he will realize that he must be careful. He will start to *think*—and some bulls are very smart.'

'See how *fuerte*—how strong he is? He lifts the horse and the rider into the air and pushes them to the wall...but the horse is protected. Here is the *pic* on his neck...and now the man with the cape comes to lure the bull away from the *picador*. Now again with the other horse. See? The bull is angry but he is starting to understand that whenever he charges the horses, he gets hurt. Do you see how he stops? He is thinking now. He is bigger and stronger, but now he must be *smarter*.'

'Now the *matador* is coming out with the *banderillas*. The bull is looking at him but he is thinking now... waiting to charge.

Five thousand years ago, and not very far from here on the island of Crete, the Minoan people played a game with giant bulls that are now—how you say?—*extinto*; none of them are alive any more. They were as tall as your father at the shoulder—great, giant beasts. When the bull would charge, they would leap up between the horns and over the bull. It was *muy peligroso*—very dangerous—but probably very exciting to see.

Now, the bull is charging the cape. The *matador* will jump out of his way and stick him with the *banderillas*."

"But he didn't jump over the bull," noted young Andreas with some disappointment.

"No…they don't do that any more. That was a long time ago…but watch the man in the yellow suit; he must be very fast and very careful to stay away from the bull's horns. He will stand behind the cape and at the moment the bull touches it, he will jump off to the side and the bull will wonder why he didn't hit anything…ah…there he goes again. See? The bull is confused. The *matador* is playing with him. *¡Que bueno!* A very nice pass.'

'Now watch him charge again. He is not using the right horn so much, now. His right side has the *banderillas* in it so he is protecting it. He is holding his head lower and not hooking so much with the right horn. It is better this way for the *matador*."

"I don't like the blood," said Andreas. "The bull is hurt."

"The bull is a very big animal," said Antonio. "It takes a lot to hurt a big bull. He is bleeding but, it just makes him mad. See how he looks at the *matador*?

And now is the best part—the *faena*—watch, Andreas...the bull charges again and again, and each time the *matador* jumps out of the way. See there? *Aii...* That was close! Very close. The bull cannot turn in a small circle like the man—he is too big—so the *matador* stays inside the bull's big circle, but he has very little to hide behind and the bull is getting smarter. Do you think the bull will figure out the *matador*'s game? If he does, it will be very dangerous for him."

The crowd roared and Andreas watched wide-eyed.

"Now, the bull is getting tired. The *matador* is walking away from him—not even looking at him—teasing him. 'Come and get me,' he says. I am just a little man with a cloth. Look...now he is on his knees with his back to the bull. The bull is just watching the *matador*. Look! He goes right up and puts a hand on the forehead of the bull...and here is the *paso*...another charge...another jump...very close...watch him spin in the air...*bonito*! Exciting, no? This is a very good bull with lots of *espíritu*. Listen to the crowd.'

'And now he is signaling for his *estoque*, the sword. It is almost finished."

"A sword?"

"He is going to kill the bull now, and if he is good,

he will do it quickly with one stroke. He does not wish to make the bull suffer…and the people will boo him if it does not happen fast. This bull has been very good."

Andreas's lip quivered. "But I don't want him to kill the bull. Why do they have to kill him?" The boy grabbed his father's hand tightly.

The *matador* held the *muleta* aloft and pointed the tip of his *estoque* at the bull dramatically.

From the edge of the ring, Hanns pointed a large telephoto lens at the *matador*'s face, catching the intensity of the moment, the steeling of the nerves to make the kill with conviction and intent, the tiny beads of perspiration on his lip, the closing of one eye and the squinting of the other to block from view anything that did not connect him with the bull before him.

The crowd cheered with anticipation.

"No!" cried Andreas.

With a wave of the *muleta*, the bull charged once more.

Andreas buried his head in his father's side.

The cheering grew louder.

"Don't let him do it, father. Don't let him…"

The bull fell to his knees…sinking…gasping blood…eyes wide with fear, rage, confusion and disbelief.

Hanns captured the *matador*'s face, carried by the moment, twisted in a strange mix of anguish, triumph and relief in the personal moment of killing—before it all became just a show again, and the bull was dead, and the man was just a paid performer, and little else remained to do but thank God for another deliverance, and bow to the cheering people with arms thrust triumphantly to the Spanish sky.

Andreas looked up just as one of the *cuadrillos* finished off the bull. The animal quivered spasmodically and rolled on his back, blood still streaming from his mouth over a twisted tongue that hung limply, staining the sand a dark crimson under the once proud, dignified and mighty, black head.

The crowd leaped to their feet and shouted approval.

Andreas screamed.

"I hope the *corrida* was as fantastic as the flying." Kalimba swung through the door of the flat. "There's plenty of controversy around it, so I'm curious to know what you thought; is it a sport or is it torture?"

"Hanns was just asking me the same thing," said Anna, "but as with many topics people get stuck debating, it's the correct framing of the question that is often the problem—not the finding of the answer. Let me give you my own take on this whole thing. Hanns, you're an engineer—a problem solver. How often do you accomplish something remarkable by solving the problem as stated?"

"What do you mean, exactly?"

"Think, for example, of when you fixed my sewing machine. A typical repairman would have seen the problem simply as a worn out part that needed to be replaced. He would have ordered the part and replaced it—which is a very effective solution—but only if we're trying to solve the most superficial problem.'

'You saw the worn part as a symptom, as a weak link in a larger system. Instead of replacing that weak link with another weak link that would ultimately have worn out in the exact same way, you solved a much larger problem—the real problem—by asking and answering the right question.'

'People argue about whether bullfighting is an art or a sport, but don't really think much about what art and sports are. Most of the time, they're the same dance—the same story. Whether it's trying to get a ball into a goal, trying to shoot an arrow into a target, racing, rugby or tiddlywinks, sports are fundamentally a narrative dance depicting at least one of the essential absurdities—the most potent of these being the dance of human sexuality. Art can be the expression of many things, though it can be argued convincingly that at some level, all human energy is sexual energy. We humans are either *doing it*, talking about *doing it*, trying to maneuver into position to *do it* or *doing it* through metaphorical dance.'

'Someone may become a great soccer player, a great violinist, a great painter or a great bullfighter, perhaps even a great sniper—and the world will judge that person both by the outcome of their dance and the finesse with which they practice it. One of the heroes of World War One was our own Baron Manfred von Richtofen—the Red Baron. Respected by Germans and the enemy alike because of the finesse of his aerial dancing ability, he faced bullets and death in a flamboyant red, fabric-covered airplane and shot down 80 enemy planes. One could argue fairly that he was a sadist, or that he was doing his duty or that he was an artist. What do you think? You guys are pilots who can probably appreciate the artistic aspects of such a performance better than me…and it's easy enough to dismiss death in times of war unless you start looking at how many of the downed pilots were conscripted into service…but let's not go there.'

'The problem is not whether the Red Baron was an artist or an assassin, or whether bullfighting is an art or a sport. Is it faster to Düsseldorf or by train? What is the difference between a bowl of cherries? On a scale of one to ten, what is your favorite color? Do you shower in the morning or drink wine with dinner? If people spent as much time trying to find the right questions as they did answers to the wrong ones, the world would be a happier place. Like replacing an old inferior part with a new inferior part, answering the wrong question can restore functionality and keep things moving, but it doesn't contribute much to growth and progress."

"That was marvelous," said Hanns. "Let's see…we covered bullfighting, a variety of sports, the nature of art, the Red Baron, and sewing machine repair—probably

I've forgotten a few others—all chained together in the service of problem solving theory."

"But I'm not making fun of you. I'm listening and interested—just amused and impressed at the same time. Do continue…"

Anna laughed. "So…hmm…bullfighting…or rather, *toreo*…where were we?"

"Looking for questions in all the wrong places?"

"Yes…so first off, let's give the Spaniards their due. They do not call this bull *fighting*. They call it *toreo* which basically translates as 'about the bull.' The people who practice this tradition do not call it a 'sport' and they do not call it a 'fight.' That label has been ironed on by the very people—mostly foreigners—who the *aficionados* of *toreo* claim do not understand their tradition. In fairness, regardless of what we may ultimately conclude about it, we should try to resist having our judgement tainted by someone else's name-calling."

"I'll buy that," said Hanns. "Good observation."

"So, our question becomes simply 'What is *toreo*?' and clearly, as with many other things, it is different things to different people. This may be bothersome to the average idiot who is never content with a personal point of view until it is universally accepted and attributed to his authorship, but to whatever extent

I can claim enlightenment in such matters, I will take license to refine the question further; what do *I* think about *toreo*?'

'And you know me well enough by now to know I will explain it in terms of it being a dance about sexuality.'

'The bullring—a large circle full of people— is genesis; the egg. Symbolically, every observer is a participant and collectively, they represent the random offspring that can spring forth from a sexual union. The Roman Colliseum, the Shakespearean theater and many other places of sacrifice or theatrical performance are roundly configured this way.'

'Act I: The young man comes of age and enters the world of sexuality. The bull, like the young man, is out of control. He races furiously around the ring, charging at anything that moves. Mythologically, he, or rather, his overpowering sexuality is "the beast."'

'Then, the horses come in—horses being another large, strong, hairy animal, but one which is friendly, obedient and domesticated. The horse is mounted and under control of a rider with a *pic* or lance, a symbol I doubt you need help understanding. This is idealized adult sexuality—animal urges mastered and kept completely under control. The bull charges the horses and, until the practice was banned in the late 1920's, he literally mutilated them. I'm grateful the horses today wear protection, but I can understand why they were originally an important part of the sacrifice ritual…"

"Sacrifice ritual?" asked Kalimba.

"Of course. People have sacrificed bulls to their Gods since long before biblical times and in many cases, the behaviors of these Gods paralleled the essential absurdities of human behavior. You're not going to get a stadium full of Catholics to cop on to a pagan ritual like sacrifice any more than you'll get them to give up Christmas trees or the Easter Bunny, but human spirituality ultimately happens at a part of the brain that is less concerned about what color a metaphor is than whether it fits. Stories of religion and mythology create bridges between the rational and the spiritual that help to reconcile the literal with the abstract. Most people won't find everything they need to plan their dinner in one place, so they pick a favorite and don't worry too much if the appetizers and desserts come from different recipe books…as long as those side dishes offer stories, characters and practices that feel right.'

'Animal sacrifice is mentioned in the bible, and though religion prescribes less ritual slaughter today, the eating of pigs, cows, turkeys, and other animals is associated with almost every holiday of political or spiritual significance. The old literature talks more about the actual sacrifice than its consumption but I imagine it was just as much a path to a holiday dinner then as today. Earlier cultures just made as big a deal about the killing part as the eating part—and some argue that from a spiritual perspective, consciously presiding over the death of your food is an important part of understanding your own mortality and the larger consequences of your actions.'

'So, yes, it is a sacrifice ritual. Any questions?"

"No," laughed Kalimba. "I wouldn't question a witch doctor on her psychosexual mythology.'

'You were telling us about the horses…"

"The horses…," continued Anna. "Ah, yes. The bull is too strong for the horses. He charges them and destroys them if he can…but the *picadores*, the riders lance his neck. They injure him and they anger him. They make him bleed.'

'Until this moment, it has never occurred to the bull that anything could threaten or hurt him. He is, in his own mind, omnipotent and invincible. Now, quite literally, it occurs to the bull that he must think and strategize. Symbolically, it is the beginning of the struggle between rational forces and untamed libido.'

"In Act II, the *banderilleros* lance the bull again, but the *banderillas*—the little spears—have barbs on them and the darts stay attached to the bull. In the *corrida*, the goal of Act II is to tire the bull and get him to lower his head. This has plenty of practical value to the *matador* who has to deal with an enraged bull as part of his performance. Keeping the horns down makes them less dangerous and by the way, they're probably where the term "horny" originated, but if the bull represents sexuality, the lowering of the head is not a very difficult-to-decipher piece of symbolism.'

'Additionally, we have a repeating of the penetration theme. There's a reason the *picadores* in Act I use a spear that has no barb."

"And," interjected Hanns, "there's a flat area behind the point of the *pic* that prevents it from penetrating very far. It helps to keep the bull from being severely injured too early in the *corrida*."

"Unfortunately for us women, many societies expect we should all be virgins, that we should bleed all over the bed to prove it and give men some sort of symbolic satisfaction of having killed something with their 'swords.' The popular mythology also suggests there should be at least a half-dozen virgins for every man… but let's not get lost there…themes of penetration are no great mystery and neither is the phallic symbolism of swords. I won't burden you with explanations here, but maybe it's safe to say we women have a way of getting under your skin and staying there?

The bull emerges from Act II with the *banderillas* attached; colorful darts with flowers and ribbons on them. Sounds feminine, doesn't it? Like little British flags on the side of the Red Baron's plane, the *banderillas* signify the conquests of the young man—his sexual experience—but he is tired and frustrated. He has found neither lasting satisfaction nor accomplished mastery over his sexual urges…and maybe he has been wounded, too? Perhaps he has fallen in love and experienced rejection?'

'And then we get to Act III. Here is where the *matador* must be a masterful narrator and a masterful puppeteer. His puppet is the *muleta*, the cape—which is the symbolic skirt of the young woman. During the *faena* which is the final dance, the bull charges at the cape over and over, and the *matador* teases the bull with the *muleta*. It is an enactment of the fundamental battle between masculine power and feminine allure. As in real life, each wishes to dominate the other. It is a dance which has elements of savagery and elements of affection. The *matador* and the bull appear to dance together. The male sexuality is brutish but the woman makes him dance gracefully. As a couple, they take dangerous chances and attempt to subdue each other. This enactment of the courtship ritual can make a bullfight appear powerful or merely contrived to the onlookers. They want to experience the drama, the danger, the exposure and the absurdity of the courtship dance. If the *matador* is afraid or uses a lot of cheap theatrics, the *aficionados* are disappointed. They want to see romance—not a bar room pickup.'

'Because of the duality of the symbolism, the relationship is always consummated. The matador kills the bull, or it may be that the bull gores the *matador*, in which case there is also penetration and blood. Usually, the bull stands there exhausted until the *matador* provokes a final charge and places the sword between its shoulder blades. Regardless, we have the symbolism of penetration between the legs, and the death of the beast which is metaphorically so threatening to the rule of rational thought.'

'Especially here in a Catholic country where sexual sublimation is an integral part of the spiritual landscape, the conquering of sexual energy is particularly meaningful. People are told not to masturbate, not to think about sex, not to engage in sex before marriage—

all of which are instructions that run contrary to basic human nature. Few succeed at living up to these ideals, and many are made to feel as if they have somehow failed or sinned and must beg forgiveness. Within these religious traditions, the person who successfully conquers the bull is a hero, which explains why the tradition of *toreo* is so important to so many people here and yet, is simply thought of as "bull fighting" by outsiders."

"But isn't it simpler than all that?" asked Kalimba. "I like your analysis and I don't have much ground to question it, but the theme may be as simple as "Man versus Nature."'

'People climb mountains and cross deserts. They clear away forests to build houses. When I jump in the water to spear fish, is it not unlike a *corrida* in that I might fall prey to a shark but probably will find my dinner? Isn't the drama of survival as powerful as the struggle between reason and libido?"

"Yes," said Hanns, "but I'm not sure if symbolically, that struggle is really any different from the one Anna is describing. I've been out sailing by myself on a day when the sky is blue and the waves are just right. The land is falling behind the horizon, and the boat is flying along with the rail almost in the water.

–231–

The rigging is humming. You're totally in the moment; just being one with the world, and *boing*—where did that hard-on come from? There's no erotic daydreaming that sets it off. You're entirely in the supreme moment and all of a sudden…you're ready for action."

Kalimba laughed. "I thought that only happened to me."

Anna smiled. "Let's face it…most of the owner's manuals for our sexual equipment are either cryptic, outdated or wrong."

"Doesn't that suggest," continued Hanns, "that some psychospiritual link exists between the struggle between man and nature, and the struggle between man and his *own* nature?"

"Procreation certainly crosses some borders there," suggested Anna. "It's pretty easy to argue that courtship and mating are an important part of our survival dance. That mountain may represent a world to be conquered or a mate to be conquered or an urge to be conquered, but they're all essentially the same mountain."

"From a biological point of view, it makes more sense to have the bull goring everything in site," said Hanns. "More uncomplicated fucking means more babies, which gives the species a statistically greater chance of survival."

"Not necessarily true," said Kalimba. "I have heard of places where during the winter time, people are encouraged to go out and hunt as many deer as they can because there are too many of them to find food. The mercy killing keeps them all from starving to death in the cold. Bigger populations aren't necessarily the key to survival. Look at the threats from human population growth today."

"True," acknowledged Hanns, "but uncontrolled procreation made sense when the conditions were such as during the dark ages when plagues and wars and diseases we can pop a pill for today were wiping out whole populations at a time."

"Which brings us back to the essential absurdities," said Anna. "We have a survival instinct that includes urges to compete and procreate, but we are also deeply imbued with a desire to understand our connections to other people and our connections to the Universe. Take a look at almost any traditional path to religious or spiritual understanding and you'll find that our primal programming is considered to be a direct impediment to enlightenment. Normal and natural urges to mate and compete are seen as obstacles that must be transcended before the student can become a master. As often as not, this battle looms so large that successful transcendence of baser motivations is seen as enlightenment itself.'

'So, we struggle with our dual nature. We compete for the right to mate with the most attractive partners, and we kill and sublimate the environment in order to feed and shelter ourselves and our offspring…and yet, we are able to stand apart from these instinctive practices to seek meaning and to explore the very context in which we find things to be meaningful."

"And that is…?" asked Kalimba.

"Essentially the search for love. Love is as abstract as any other spiritual state or spiritual force, and comes in as many forms and depictions. Love is intangible; we can produce no empirical evidence for its existence, yet we clearly experience it.'

'To finally answer the question then, what I personally think about *toreo* is this; I think the ritual sacrifice of the bull is rather unfortunate for the bull, but I can see why it resonates so powerfully within the cultures that practice it. Repressed sexual urges that go unvented can be dangerous, and it may be that *toreo* serves as an outlet for some people that could possibly even reduce sexual crime. It's a barbaric thing to intentionally inflict pain, but I doubt that any less fear or suffering occurs when an antelope is killed by a lion on the African plains. Violence is fundamental to nature.

I'm saddened that people need this, but you won't find me out walking with the protesters. Evolution is not a glamorous process, and I'll pick my battles.'

'I do believe that as a drama, *toreo* answers the wrong question. You can argue compellingly that mastery over sexual desire is a prerequisite for finding love and meaning. All those meaningless sexual experiences often lead a more mature person to seek "something more" within the context of a relationship. Maybe this is why *aficionados* will sit through six *corridas* in a single afternoon? I don't know, but the ridiculous suggestion that sexuality *can* or *should* be conquered does a lot of cultural, emotional and spiritual damage in the world.'

'Have you ever met people who just stank of "adulthood?" People who are stiff, formal, disciplined and gray? People who rarely laugh and just have nothing childlike about them?"

"Personally," said Hanns, "I feel like a big kid. I play with big-boy toys, but I do take care of my bills and all the other mundane stuff that just has to be done in the service of living life in the land of clocks and calendars."

"Exactly," said Anna,"which is why you're both wonderful and insufferable at the same time."

Kalimba chuckled at the friendly barb.

"My point is that adulthood is not something that *replaces* childhood—it's something that *augments* childhood. Curiosity, wonder, playfulness and mischievousness are all as innate as the mating instinct, but we see how drab people become when they lose their childlike qualities.'

'The search for love and meaning is not predicated on *conquering* the bull. It depends more on *accepting* the bull as a part of our own nature. The actual killing of the bull is, for me, a rather unfortunate piece of symbolism because it leads people down an endless path that can't ultimately be very satisfying—a compelling answer to another wrong question."

"But in order to find love and meaning within the context of a relationship, it has to be about more than just sex," challenged Kalimba. "If the bull is there, it has to be sublimated in some way, no?"

"Yes. Which is why in spite of my objections to its naive spiritual picture, I do think *toreo* is an art."

"But how can pagan ritual slaughter be considered an art?"

"Paint. Play guitar. Write a poem. Walk on a high wire. Shoot an arrow at a target; and remember what the center of the target is called. Climb a mountain. Swim across a river. Kill a bull with a sword. What is any art but the abstract expression of sublimated sexual energy?'

'In fact I can find only one really compelling reason to judge it harshly."

"And that is…?"

"We spoke of childhood and adulthood. My son was clearly fascinated by the bull and the horses. He was concerned for the horses, but realized they weren't being hurt and then continued to enjoy the *corrida*. He got fidgety when they darted the bull and I could see him squeezing Tino's hand when he saw the blood, but with everyone around him enjoying the show, he didn't complain. When the *matador* came on and danced with the bull, he was mesmerized—and it was undeniably a beautiful and exciting performance—but when he realized the *matador* was going to kill the bull, he looked away. When he looked up and saw the animal fall to its knees gasping blood, he was horrified.'

'Children can become acculturated to the most extreme violence when conditions are sufficiently harsh. We all have to process what we see in order to survive and move on, no matter how young we are; but a basic quality of civilized society is reverence for childhood. We try to create an environment where children can play games, ask their questions and explore their world at a pace that allows them to experience the simple joys of youth. We let them believe in fairies and elves and Santa Clause with the knowledge that some day, they will have to grow up, abandon their fairy tale beliefs, and deal with the practicalities of survival and the essential absurdities—not that the "Christ and miracles" mythology of the adult world is really any more empirically credible than the fat guy with the flying reindeer who brings presents down your chimney—but that's a different subject.'

'A child who has never been exposed to something before sees it for the first time in a certain way, I'm inclined to give some credence to that perspective. It's often naive and often part of the inevitable shock of discovering the real world, but it's definitely uncolored. Children's perspectives are often among the wisest, simplest and most profound. Andreas got a taste of the World's harsh realities today—such revelations are a tragically necessary part of growing up—but it's worth meditating on whether he lost something of value today that we may all have lost and forgotten a long time ago. If a child instinctively reacts negatively towards something, I can honor that. They know far less than we do, which means in certain ways, they know far *more;* that's their magical strength.'

'To get back to *the question*, for me, *toreo* is indisputably an art—a skillful dance—but I cannot see it as a sport for anyone other than those who have not evolved beyond a point where love itself is only a sport."

Anna placed Andreas up on the wing and held his hand as he stepped into the door of the sleek, silver aircraft. "Hanns, thank you for flying us down. I wish we had more time to stay and explore, but it's been a most inspiring adventure." She winked at him. "I'm looking forward to having more time to visit when you get back to Germany, so don't stay away too long."

Tino embraced his wife before she grabbed the black leather strap hanging above the entrance way and swung herself up into the plane.

"It's been a pleasure," said Kalimba, his sunglasses on and his pilot's headphones around his neck. "I'm so glad to have been a part of this circus of yours. Call me when you're done with the show and I'll fly you guys back to *Deutschland*. I don't want to miss hearing the end of the story when we're so close to it."

"And how do you know that?" asked Hanns.

"Just a feeling. I think I'll be seeing you soon enough. Cheers, and give Antonio my wishes for best of luck with his *corrida*."

The cockpit door eased down with a motorized whir and locked. Hanns grabbed the chocks from under the tires, placed them behind the rear seat of the plane, and shot a final smile at Anna and Andreas who were putting on their harnesses. Andreas looked particularly pleased to have a full-sized set of pilot's headphones with a microphone boom on. Hanns shut the passenger door, and Kalimba cranked the starboard engine over; the propeller began to rotate and the whirring of turbines grew quickly into a roar. The port engine followed in similar style, and the grinning pilot shot Hanns a final salute.

Hanns and Tino retreated to the comparative quiet of the Citröen's cabin, joining Antonio and Vanessa who had already climbed in back.

An outrageous orgy of red and chrome, the plane taxied a short distance, paused for clearance at the beginning of the runway and then screamed off into the blue Andalusian sky like a crimson meteor.

"Next stop, *Ronda*," said Hanns. "I'm looking forward to seeing it. We can add to our list of great coincidences the fact that Tino's guitar quest has pointed us to that very same place. Whether or not fate is in operation here, it's sure damned convenient."

Vanessa held Antonio's hand, which made his whole body stiffen up. She let it go when it began to sweat.

A half-hour down the road, she placed a hand

on Hanns's shoulder and made a comment about his "beautiful hair," but he had no intention of being pulled into the romantic drama unfolding in the back seat. He politely and cleverly let the gesture slide off in a way that indicated his clear disinterest to Antonio, and offered little foothold for Vanessa to contrive offense or inspire jealousy.

To his surprise, and certainly to Vanessa's, Antonio had actually invited her to join him on the *Ronda* trip. Typically, Vanessa would have been the one trying to corner Antonio in some romantic place with a big bed in a small hotel room, but it made some sense to bring a fair damsel along to cheer for her champion in the arena. The wisdom of bringing potential conflict anywhere near one's first big *corrida* was questionable, but at very least, it might all be interesting if viewed from a safe distance.

Tino sat quietly, lost in thought.

They drove silently, making their way to the Southeast through the dry country, and then into rocky, more mountainous territory. The lurid, blue waters of the *Embalse de Zahara* glided by to their right. Hanns watched neat rows of olive groves racing hypnotically along in a twirling dance of perspective. White Moorish villages with red tile roofs appeared on the hillsides—

mirages visiting from a time seven centuries before. The air cooled as the elevation grew higher.

"It's hard to believe things can be so different an hour-and-a-half out of *Sevilla*," noted Hanns. "I bet it's looked the same way for a thousand years. From what I hear, *Ronda* has the same ancient flavor. Have you been there before, Antonio?"

"Sí," replied Antonio, grateful for a chance to break the silence and hold court on a subject about which he was knowledgeable, and which didn't make him long for the confessional when the discussion was over. "I did some of my training in *Ronda* one summer.'

'It is the ancestral home of Spanish *toreo*. The *Plaza de Toros de Ronda* built in the 1780's is the oldest bullfighting arena in Spain still used today. All the seats are covered—protected from the sun, and a very famous statue of a Spanish bull stands just outside. In the old days, *toreo* was done strictly on *caballos*— on trained horses. The *Jerez* style of *toreo* is hardly practiced today, but if you get a chance to see it, it is a beautiful thing how the horse and rider work quickly and fearlessly together, as if they share one mind. It is *increíble* how the caballeros trust their lives to the horses…and how the horses trust their riders—a very different kind of dance than the *toreo* commonly seen."

Antonio paused to clarify the details of his story to Vanessa in Spanish, and then continued. "It was in *Ronda* that Pedro Romero started the tradition of facing the bull on foot, a far more dangerous game because it brings the *torero* to the same level as the horns of the bull. He started this around the same time the *Plaza de Toros de Ronda* was *construido*, and was the first *matador* to treat *toreo* as a true art. History says he retired in 1799 without a single scar on his body, after killing over 6000 bulls; though this not so easy to believe when every professional I know has a few souvenirs from his days in the *corrida*—even the very best.'

'*Ronda* is an old Moorish City built in the *montañas* on the *El Tajo* canyon which has three very old bridges crossing over it. For taking pictures, it is one of the most beautiful places in all of *España*. I know *Ronda* well and will show you some of my special places. It's not far now…and Vanessa says she has a cousin there."

"We have a line on a guitar in Ronda, too, so our first order of business will be to drop you and Vanessa at the hotel," said Hanns. "I've gotten two rooms at a nice place so you can be comfortable before your *corrida*. I want to spend a good part of tomorrow setting up to shoot, so I'm going to push forward on the guitar quest this afternoon and hopefully complete that mission; I have a good feeling about it."

The reality of a sharing a room with Antonio dawned on Vanessa who smiled mischievously, but Antonio showed little reaction. Clearly, he was thinking about his *corrida*, and Hanns made a note to discreetly suggest she wait to kill her bull until *after* Antonio had killed his.

The cross-country drive ended all too quickly. After checking in at the hotel, a light lunch on a quiet terrace overlooking the canyon provided a perfect interlude. Antonio allowed himself a glass of wine and at least for the moment, he and Vanessa looked content, gazing across the chasm with glasses in hand.

Hanns grabbed an object from his pocket and hurled it over the edge. "For luck.'

'Shall we go, Tino?"

"I suppose…yes…but…let's just go, yes."

The men left some money on the table and headed out through the door of the hotel lobby to the truck.

"I thought you were being quiet, even for you, Tino. Tell me…"

"You remember Bernard from the gypsy camp… how he asked me to come back?"

"I remember," said Hanns. "I assumed you just went out and played guitar that night…and that we were here in Ronda with information about your magic guitar-maker."

"I went back to *Triana*, played at the Club, and waited for Bernard but he never showed up. I figured I'd try to find the place myself. It's on the river, right? Once you hit the river, it might be upstream or it might be downstream, but it can't be any closer or any farther."

"Tino," Hanns interrupted with a smile. "Am I seeing a bit of the navigator in you? I didn't think you had it in you."

"When I was a boy, those of us who liked to chase the young girls had to know our escape routes in case a jealous father should appear…but let me tell you… I found the gypsy place after not too much searching and it was empty."

"What do you mean 'empty?'"

"'Empty' as in all the campers, huts and tents had disappeared; it was just a big dump littered with debris. I went up and down the block a few times to make sure I wasn't at the wrong lot, but too many things were recognizable; the poster on the fence outside and the two boards that swung open to get in. The old truck and the rusty containers were there, and the outhouse on the dock. It was very strange—just a big, dead lot with the ruins of an old building on it—a mess.'

'I poked around and finally found Bernard sitting alone on the water and staring into space. He didn't even look at me, but when I called his name, he got wild-eyed and suspicious. He clearly didn't recognize me, and when I started telling him details about his life, he started jabbering in English about how he wasn't going to let me force him to go to Vietnam.'

'I finally convinced him I was Spanish, and I tried to remind him about the gypsies and the flamenco music. It was like I had met his twin brother in a parallel universe and then…it was just weird to find him that way. Any memory of our ever having been there had disappeared with the gypsies.'

'I finally just gave him a little money and left."

"Let's just drive and see what we find," suggested Hanns, fastening his seat belt and starting up the Citröen. "At very least, there's no need to hang around the hotel and watch hormones battle against the bible. We have a beautiful place to explore. Besides…your *guitarra* may have disappeared, but Hanns's bastardization of Newton's law suggests that for every disappearance, there is an equal and opposite appearance."

"You realize, my friend," said Tino, "that this is totally fucking insane?"

"Can you think of any better reason for it to work?

Let's have some fun, stay positive and if all things are ultimately part of the larger whole, we should get ourselves out into the world where totally fucking insane connections can find us. It beats hiding in the room unless you've met some girls I don't know about."

Tino laughed and fastened his seat belt. The Citröen lurched back out onto the ancient Spanish highways. "So, are you going to tell me what it was that you threw into *El Tajo* back at lunch?"

"Nothing really—just a bag containing an old brass hammer and some pieces of splintered guitar."

The beige Citröen raced through olive groves, vineyards, and forests of Spanish fir; Hanns in his element on the winding Roads.

"Why do you cross into the oncoming lane on these curves?" asked Tino.

"Before I went to the Middle East, I used to race BMWs—1602s and 2002 TiSas. A straight line is the shortest distance between two points so you learn to chop off the curves when you can. It's a habit now, really. Also, you've known me long enough to know I'm not a person who navigates much by the lines mankind has painted on the earth."

Continuing out into the countryside, Hanns turned off onto a lesser road when the opportunity to leave the highway presented itself.

"Just an instinct," said Hanns. "I just can't envision much magic happening on the *bahn*."

Tino laughed. "I'm just along for the ride.'

'I have to admit; I'm a little surprised at you sacrificing stuff to the Canyon Gods and all that. I had you pegged as a strict rationalist. Do you have a shrine to the Blessed Virgin hidden in the back of the truck?"

"Virgins aren't my thing, honestly—totally overrated. A little experience goes a long way and besides, the nature of virgins is that they stop being virgins the very moment you sleep with them. Maybe the whole virginity thing made sense in a time when having as many children as possible was important to keeping the species alive? Keeping fathers connected to those kids was part of a sound survival strategy, but the whole 'innocence and purity' thing is primitive and naive. I've been fucking my way around this World since I was big enough to get out and swim in it, and I can't think of anything more natural, innocent and in accordance with nature's plan. I haven't ever forced myself on anybody or lied to anyone to get them out of their clothes. I have no guilt and no sins to confess…I'm innocent…and I certainly ain't no virgin.'

'But to answer your real question about why I'm tossing offerings into the gorge, it's not something I can really wrap my head around in a conscious sense, but— and I think this is even more true for extremely rational people—the subconscious mind doesn't take much stock in whether anything makes *sense*. It believes in magic as much as it can really believe in anything; belief being a territory under the jurisdiction of the rational brain. The subconscious traffics more in hunches, feelings and intuitions than in any sort of definable beliefs.

I've seen enough coincidence and inexplicable magic in my life to wonder if thoughts aren't like some sort of gravitational field that bends reality like a black hole bends light. I don't know how or why or even *if* it really works, or if it's just wishful thinking, but if it does work, it doesn't work on a conscious level. If it did, we'd live in a chaotic collision of billions of personal realities. Who knows? Maybe that's why the world is such a crazy place? But we seem to have our own spiritual gravity fields capable of capturing certain people and objects into orbit around us. You and I collided in a park two weeks ago and are now trekking across Andalusia together.'

'I don't consciously believe in any sentient force that is going to be honored by my offering of an old greasy hammer, deem me worthy and shower me with things I desire. But subconsciously, I know I've given up something meaningful—meaning itself coming from outside the logical brain. That was my grandfather's hammer. When there's a sense something special has been lost, that creates an openness to receiving something to fill that vacuum. It's a possible mechanism for turning on the reality-bending gravity field—and *meaning* seems to have a lot to do with it. If I'm desperate to make a phone call, I'll find a coin on the street, but the subconscious mind doesn't get excited about a million *deutschmarks* or a new sports car. They're desirable but not meaningful.'

'I don't honestly think traditional prayer or sacrifice works any differently, but most people see God as an entirely external force. Traditional religion is mostly about disconnected people trying to reconnect with God. I don't believe in external, intelligent deities but I do believe we're all vessels for something very powerful. Maybe this force is collective and manifests itself through each of us? Maybe we each have our own internal, spiritual battery pack? I don't know or care, or worry about whether it's rational or not—or even true. As long as there's magic and mystery in my life, I don't need to run around denying it to preserve my picture of myself as a rational being. The subconscious mind is a powerful thing, and many of our rational actions are carried out in the service of pursuing its abstract, emotional and spiritual ends. '

'For you, playing the guitar expresses a spiritual voice of the subconscious, and has deep, personal meaning. For me, *finding* you a guitar is a task assumed by the rational mind. On some level, it's just a material pursuit—a desire. I have no deep-seated urge to express myself by teasing the strings. By tossing my grandfather's hammer into the gorge, I'm attempting to invoke the powers of the subconscious mind by introducing a new level of personal meaning to my mission. It's a cheap trick, really. I tossed the hammer and the guitar fragments not because it makes any rational sense, but to subconsciously connect the search for your guitar to something personally, deeply meaningful.'

'The subconscious does talk to us. We don't always listen, but it's voice can be heard in art, music, fantasies and dreams. It's not a rational voice, but it's a voice worth listening to. Most people seem bent on trying to get it to shut up, but those who encourage it to speak find it capable of listening when it feels listened to. You just have to approach it more abstractly than you would the rational mind."

"So what do you do next?" asked Tino. "Do you meditate in a certain way or try to visualize a guitar?"

"None of that. It's out of my hands—or at least consciously so where any concept of 'my' exists. Let's enjoy the cool air, drive through the olive groves and let life unfold. We've expressed our readiness and openness to embrace what comes. Our prayer has been offered and our sacrifice has been made.

The rest is up to the Universe, and that leaves the day ours to enjoy.'

'I wonder how fast this thing can go, anyway."

"Before you get a case of lead-foot, let's see if that guy can use a hand," suggested Tino, pointing to a weathered sedan parked on the shoulder.

Hanns pulled off the road behind the car and Tino leaned out the open window. *"¿Quieres ayuda?"*

The man waved a red gas can. *"Gracias. Necesito petróleo. Hay un estacion de gasolina en dies kilometros. Si posible…"*

"Out of gas," explained Tino. "He says there's a station about ten kilos up the road."

"Vamos…no problemo," called Tino opening his door to let the man in.

"Muchas Gracias," said the man, climbing into the back seat with his empty gas can.

Tino explained that they were looking for a guitar-maker as they drove on through the olive groves. The farmer listened quietly. About sixty, his dark hair was streaked with gray; his face was wrinkled and dark from years of toil under the Spanish sun.

He nodded his head and shrugged. They filled his jug at the station and drove him back to his car where he thanked them with two green bottles of olive oil.

They waved and drove off. Tino looked discouraged.

"Let's stop for a drink in *Yunquera* up ahead," suggested Hanns. "I'm thirsty and want to stretch a bit."

Tino shrugged.

"And here it is!" exclaimed Hanns.

"Where?"

Hanns turned up a dirt driveway. "A tiny sign on the mail box: *Guitarras.*"

They parked in front of a small, white, typically Spanish house with a red tile roof and went to the door.

There was no answer.

"I thought this might be it," said Tino with some disappointment in his voice.

"Maybe it is. Read the card on the door. What does it say?"

Fine Instruments and Repairs
Señor Ernesto de la Luz, *Ronda.*

Pulling out of the driveway and back onto the main road, they headed back towards *Ronda* and soon saw a flashing of headlights ahead.

"It's the man we helped with the fuel," said Tino. "He's waving for us to stop."

The two cars pulled over and Tino got out to speak

with the man briefly before getting back into the car. "He said he found this in his car…not a clue where it came from. It looks like one of those scraps of paper that ends up riding under the seat with the old receipts and gum wrappers."

"I wouldn't know about those," laughed Hanns, "but what does it say?"

Fine Instruments and Repairs
Señor Ernesto de la Luz, *Ronda*.

A wild ride through the Olive groves soon had Hanns parking the Citröen on the street in front of the hotel. Antonio and Vanessa sat in the lobby talking with a vibrant, mid-thirtyish man who smiled warmly, gesturing dramatically and passionately as he spoke.

"Tino…Hanns…Come here," said Antonio noting his friends' return. "I want for you to meet the cousin of Vanessa…"

Hanns and Tino stepped over and politely took the man's hand.

Hanns bowed his head respectfully and then turned to Tino. "Please beg his forgiveness for a quick visit, but we don't have much time left to find your man in *Ronda*…"

"No need for translations, and no offense taken if you are in a hurry," returned Vanessa's cousin. "Who is it you are looking for here in *Ronda*? Maybe I know him? It is not such a big place."

Tino handed over the faded card. "Ernesto de la Luz... Ernesto de la Luz...Where have I heard that name before?"

Vanessa and Antonio grew wide-eyed.

"Ah yes, I remember now," smiled the man calmly. He reached into his pocket, withdrew a billfold and removed a card, handing it to Tino.

Fine Instruments and Repairs
Señor Ernesto de la Luz, *Ronda*.

"No need to rush, my friends. *Ronda* has waited a thousand years for you to arrive, and here you are. Have faith. The people and things you seek will come to you in their time.'

'Freshen up. Have a *cerveza*. Enjoy some *tapas*. Tell me about your music, and afterwards, we'll go over to my workshop which is at the same address as this hotel, one street over."

Tino looked dumbfounded. Hanns adopted the smug look of someone whom circumstances had favored with being right, and Antonio and Vanessa got a good chuckle over Tino's expression.

"But how is it that we found your card tacked to the door of a house way out near *Yunquera*?" asked Hanns.

"I had a student who tried the guitar business for a while but then found an opportunity to train as a technician of some sort—sewing machines, I think it was. He went to Germany to study and probably left my cards on his door to refer his old customers my way."

"Let's start over. I am Hanns, and this is Tino who will be capable of excellent conversation once he recovers his powers of speech."

Ernesto shook their hands once again, filled two glasses with red, Spanish wine and raised his glass. "A toast…to finding one's way."

Smells of cedar and shellac embraced them as they stepped off the cobblestone sidewalk into Ernesto's shop; a simple, narrow, open room with work benches up and down the sides and a small table in the middle. On the wall adjacent to the door hung a small collection of instruments with hand-written tags noting what work had or was to be done to them. A wooden display case with glass panels containing the traditional assortment of strings, straps, capos, music books and cassettes crossed the room, effectively partitioning off the work area from the customer area; an old yellow and red *muleta* hung on a string across the gap between the wall and the display case, serving as a simple gate.

Ernesto locked the door and flipped the window sign around so it read "*cerrado*" to passers-by. "Let me get some stools to sit on and a few instruments.'

'Tino, do you prefer a *blanca* or a *negra*?"

"The guitar I lost was a *blanca*—very plain and light as a feather—but I prefer to let my ears do the choosing. I don't really care what the guitar is made of or what it looks like. I am looking for a certain voice."

"Let's start with a *blanca,* then. This one is

extremely light, responsive and a completely traditional instrument. You may notice it has friction pegs instead of gears? Tuning gears add weight. A flamenco guitar is percussive and by reducing mass, I reduce sustain. Though they make the instrument slightly more difficult to tune, violin players have used friction pegs for years."

"My old *guitarra* had tuning pegs, too. I'm quite used to them, actually." Tino tapped on the guitar's top and closed his eyes. He smelled the varnish and the freshly-sanded wood.

"I finished that one just a few weeks ago," explained the luthier. "You are really the first one to play it; you may even hear it start to open up as you play."

Tino started at the bottom and played a run up to the high frets, then strummed some chords, starting softly and building in volume to test the dynamic range of the guitar. "A wonderful instrument. I have been playing some very fine guitars here in Spain, some of which are very old and formerly owned by famous *flamencos*. This guitar is in league with the best of them, but I am still missing a special voice—a voice I've only ever heard in the guitar I lost and surprisingly, in a few guitars I heard at a gypsy camp."

Hanns grabbed his camera and captured the

late afternoon light playing on Tino's face and the pale yellow top of the guitar.

"Here's another;" offered Ernesto, "made from the same wood taken from the same tree. The only difference is the veneer on the peghead."

Tino played again for a moment. "It's fascinating how two children from the same parents can be so different, isn't it? This one's wonderful, too, but moodier, darker, a bit less cooperative but in a desirable, mischievous way."

"You have an excellent ear…and you play as well as Antonio and Vanessa told me you did. Let me take this one from you so you can try one of my *negras*."

Tino carefully returned the instrument to its maker.

"*Negras* are traditionally made from Brazilian Rosewood—which is very hard, dense wood. Some people like the dramatic look of the swirly grain patterns you see when it is slab-cut, but I will only build with perfectly straight-grained wood. It is much plainer, but I think of wood grain as a collection of little musical tubes. Ideally, guitar wood is quartersawn—cut so the tubes run unbroken, side-by-side. This uniformity reduces the chances of the back or sides cracking as the humidity rises and falls and the guitar expands and contracts over the years.

This particular guitar is made from African Blackwood—another rosewood that is slightly denser than the Brazilian variety and much rarer. Blackwood grows on the African savannah. It's generally not very big and tends not to grow very straight. One tree in a thousand is big and straight enough to make well-quartered guitar backs from, though it's frequently used for clarinets. The Africans call it *mpingo*—the music tree. It is a beautiful, dark chocolate brown—almost like ebony—and it turns almost black when polished. I've left a little bit of bright yellow sapwood along the center seam. This wood offers a wonderful chance to build for good tone and good looks at the same time.'

'Most makers are far too traditional to build with anything exotic, but my father always loved this wood. He was always experimenting, and told me to think of every tradition as nothing more than an innovation that succeeded. He was always pushing in new directions and honored tradition by expanding on it.

'Here…see what you think."

Tino took the instrument and sat it on his knee. "It's heavy."

"Yes, the Blackwood is very dense, but it has a tremendous ring to it. Play."

Tino ran his fingers up and down the fretboard.

"It's tremendously complex—much different than the cypress-bodied guitars, yet there is still something distinctly flamenco about it. It's not the sound I've been looking for, but it's a sound I like—something different."

Ernesto smiled. "Play it for a year and it will open up like a fine wine. The problem with playing brand new guitars is that it's like looking at babies and trying to predict which will win a beauty contest twenty years later. Some faces will give you more hints than others, but only time will really tell. With guitars, the best you can do is start off with an instrument that shows promise when it is still green. From there, it is a matter of learning that instrument's voice and how to express yourself through it while that voice matures. A great guitar and a great *tocaor* ultimately grow into their sound together."

"Do you have any older or used instruments; maybe one of your own that has been played in?" asked Tino. "I'd just like to compare."

"Two weeks ago, a man made me an offer I couldn't refuse for a personal guitar I'd been playing for several years, but I do have a guitar made by my father that you would be more than welcome to try."

Ernesto got up and unlocked a cabinet in the back

of the shop, opened the door and grabbed a rather plain cypress guitar. He plucked a string on one of the guitars hanging on the shop wall as he walked forward, tuning the guitar in his hands to the note's memory as he brought it to the front. It was in fairly good condition, but showed signs of wear on the top and fingerboard.

"I learned to make guitars from my father starting when I was just a kid running around his shop begging him to teach me. This is the very last guitar he made before he died. Every instrument I build is still made with his tools and techniques—along with a few tricks I've developed on my own."

Tino struck a single chord and savored the sound long after it had disappeared. A sad smile flickered across his face.

Then he began to play.

Music swirled around the room as a tear trickled from his eye. Hanns stopped shooting photographs and looked at Ernesto who mouthed the word "*Duende*" to him as he sat enraptured on the stool. Tino continued and Ernesto began to weep silently. Even Hanns felt the corner of his mouth tighten up; his eyes misted. The room spun, and Hanns grabbed his stool for balance. The music ebbed and flowed like a new-moon tide under a clear, starry sky.

Tino stopped and stared at the instrument for a moment before beginning again.

Hanns pulled off his boot, withdrew a roll of cash and began counting bills onto the top of the display case.

Ernesto held his temples between the thumb and middle finger of his right hand, and nodded his head painfully from side to side. Hanns put more money on the table and looked Ernesto in the eye.

Tino continued to play.

Ernesto clenched his fists.

"Stop," he said. "Stop…I am sorry to stop the music, but I cannot do this.'

'This guitar is one of the last memories I have of my dear father who was murdered by the government years ago. He was an accomplished *flamenco* and when I hear this guitar played in this way, it is like he is in the room with us. I have heard many people play this guitar but you are the first to sound like him. It is very sad and very beautiful to me, and I thank you. This is without doubt the right instrument for you.'

'I'd like to believe that with time and playing-in, one of my guitars will sound like this one, but I have no way to guarantee that. If you like, I will sell one to you at a fair price and should you ever wish to return it,

I will buy it back from you.'

'The price you offer for my father's *blanca* is beyond generous, and I could use the money, but I hope you will understand why I cannot part with the very last *guitarra de mi padre.*"

One of Ernesto's tears splashed onto the glass display top next to the pile of money.

Tino was silent.

"Can you give us a moment, Ernesto?" asked Hanns. "Let me talk with Tino."

"Certainly," said the luthier whose buoyant character could not quite be defeated by his tears and memories. "I'll wait outside. Take your time."

"I know you're disappointed, "said Hanns, "but for all you know, your original *guitarra* was made by Ernesto's father and…"

"I'm certain of it. It was almost like playing my old *guitarra* again—not exactly the same but the same like identical twins are the same—very close but with subtle differences. In ways, this guitar is even *better* than my old one and in other ways, not. I can't believe we've finally found it and it's not for sale."

"Let me make a suggestion," said Hanns. "Our friend here has the right pedigree, uses the same tools and techniques and has a sincerity about him that is genuine and undeniable. Why don't you pick your favorite of his available guitars and take him up on his offer? Either the new guitar will open up, or you'll eventually find another one you like better and return this one. You have nothing to lose and you may end up with a masterpiece. If you ever want to upgrade, my offer will remain good—the guitar will be my gift to you.'

'We are running out of time here, and I worry we'll get back to Germany empty-handed. You said these were very fine guitars. Can you be happy with one of these…at least for now?"

Tino thought for a second.

"Hanns, we drove halfway across Spain today just to find two cards that pointed us right back to *Ronda*, only to find the very person we were looking for was a block away, and that that person just happened to be the cousin of one of the people we brought with us.'

'Your reasons are very practical, but I'm going to switch places with you. I'm actually more afraid that if I walk away now, I'll be ignoring something powerful and special. You know I'm not usually one who listens to those kinds of voices, but today, they are screaming at me."

Hanns opened the door and motioned for Ernesto

to come back in.

"*Señor* de la Luz," began Tino, "I would like to buy one of your guitars. If I were to take one of the *blanca*s, I would always be comparing it in my mind to my old *guitarra*—which I am certain was made by your father. That would be an injustice to us both. The *negra* has a different voice—beautiful and undoubtedly flamenco—but different. I would be proud to own it, and will look forward to discovering what music it likes to make. If I cannot have my beautiful old voice back, I will find a beautiful new one."

Ernesto grabbed the chocolate-bodied guitar and placed it in a case along with a few sets of strings. "It is my gift to you, Tino. I ask only that you return some day to play it for me, and that when people ask about it, you give them the name of de la Luz.'

'I will come out well with this arrangement. You performing on my instrument is all the marketing I will ever need. Write me after a while and let me know how the guitar opens up for you. Send me a recording if you can. I'd be honored and so would my father."

The two men embraced and it was done.

Hanns helped Antonio put on his red *traje de luces*, the *matador*'s traditional "suit of lights" covered with gold brocade. Vanessa poked her head into the dressing room and exclaimed *"¡Que bonito!"* before Veronica, who had arrived that morning, ushered her away per Hanns's strict instructions.

"If you feel as good as you look," said Hanns, "the bull is going to run the moment he sees you."

"I am nervous but I am ready," said Antonio, crossing himself. "Were you able to get the cameras set up as you wanted?"

"Yes…yes. I'm all ready, too. You have your *traje de luces* for bulls and I have my press credentials for bullshit. Everyone who needs to be impressed has either been paid off or lied to."

Antonio laughed.

"Take these," said Hanns, handing Antonio his aviator's glasses. "I want to take some photographs of you before *la corrida* starts."

Already, a few tourists and *toreo aficionados* were arriving in hopes of finding choice seats before the crowds came. The sun was still high and the stands were shaded. A cool mountain breeze mixed with the heat rising from the sands of the *plaza de toros* and stirred the ancient dust.

"These *novillero corrida*s are different from the professional ones in *Sevilla*. The professional circuit attracts big crowds, but in many ways, it is more controlled and more staged. People come to big *corrida*s expecting to be entertained. Sometimes the bulls are chosen for their show characteristics rather than for their ferocity. In the *novillero corrida*s, people don't come for flashy showmanship—they come to see a man confront a bull. Real *aficionados* sometimes prefer to watch *novilleros* perform in places like *Torremolinos* and here in *Ronda*. There is less money involved, and not so much perception that the *torero* is a celebrity entertainer. I have friends who are *matadores* on the professional circuit, and they tell me their days as *novilleros* were the most challenging of their careers. The bulls are sometimes bigger and more dangerous, and when you win, you make very little money. It is a testing ground, but it is authentic Spanish *toreo*. For me, it is a chance to step up to the next level."

"Do you get to see the bulls before the *corrida*?" asked Hanns. "How do you know which bulls you will fight?"

"Let's go see the *toros* now," suggested Antonio. "As in the professional matches, three *matadores* will each fight two bulls. I am the newcomer so I will be first to perform, but my bulls will be chosen by a drawing of numbers. That part is all up to God."

Hanns and Antonio looked down into a holding area where each of the huge animals was kept in a small enclosure. Some stood passively, and others butted angrily at the partitions, clearly annoyed at being closed-in and unhappy about the change from familiar surroundings.

Antonio pointed to a chalk board where the names and weights of the bulls were listed. "These are big bulls; Miuras. Typical fighting bulls are three-quarters this size."

Hanns snapped a few photographs and pointed his movie camera down at the animals. Better views could be had, but not from any vantage point worth risking one's neck over.

"I assume bigger bulls are more dangerous?"

"A big bull has greater strength, but his greater size limits his turning ability. His greater weight also makes it more difficult for him to stop quickly, but he will be harder to wear down, and even when he lowers his head, the horns will be higher than on a smaller bull.

I am not so worried about a big bull as an intelligent one. Each *corrida* is only fifteen minutes long for a reason. It doesn't give the bull too much time to get smart. When a bull figures out why nothing is there when he charges the *muleta*, it is very dangerous for the *matador*."

Hanns took photographs of the *matador*s and *cuadrillos* preparing for the *corrida* as they smoked and talked among themselves. He waved his press credentials and walked out into the ring to shoot wide-angle views of the stands, and then returned to Antonio's side. "Where are the horses?"

"Often, *novilleros* perform *sin picadores*. There was no money for horses and extra people, as it was spent on getting the very best bulls. I like being around the horses, but it is not to be this time. I am sorry. I would have liked for you to film them."

Antonio looked confident; Hanns's sunglasses transformed him. His body language was relaxed. He was ready. It was time.

The light was right and the weather was perfect. This was going to be Antonio's big day, and Hanns already had film footage racing through his mind's eye. Tino had proven utterly useless as a camera operator, but Veronica had picked up the workings of the movie camera quickly. She took her position at a part of the ring opposite where Hanns stood with a second camera and a press pass Hanns had not had the heart to tell her was phony. "No liar is so convincing," he thought, "than one who does not know she is lying." Hanns had not wanted to burden Antonio with extraneous concerns about lighting, angles and positioning, but there was no telling exactly where, in the large ring, the action would take place. Two cameras with good zoom lenses would have to do the job. It would all come together. Everything else had.

He checked in with Veronica on a walkie-talkie. *"¿Como estás, amor?* Are you having fun yet?"

The walkie-talkie hissed briefly. "You realize I'm doing the last thing I want to be doing in the last place I want to be doing it? I'm doing this for you and Antonio, but you are going to suffer great indignities at my hands."

"Attitude. Attitude," teased Hanns in return. "Remember, your job is to seek out tiny moments of elegance, beauty and the suspension of natural laws. Reach out through the lens with your eye and your heart and draw these moments back into the film." He pointed his zoom lens at Veronica who saw him and took advantage of the moment to stick out her tongue at him. "Got that," chuckled Hanns. "Over and out."

The stands continued to fill, and Antonio came by one last time to shake Hanns's hand and blow a kiss to Vanessa who sat in a box of seats with Tino and Ernesto de la Luz. "Thank you for this, *amigo*. The next time you see me, I will be in the *corrida*."

Hanns smiled silently.

The band struck up the Spanish National anthem followed by traditional *pasodoble*. Without horses, the small group of *cuadrillos* circled the ring briefly and without great fanfare, possibly hoping not to appear to the crowd to in any way regard themselves worthy of categorization as a "parade."

A moment later, the crowd cheered again as the first bull was released into he ring. Hanns had not seen it in the holding area, but recognized it instantly as the white bull that had stared at him at the Miura ranch. Hanns pushed the send button on the walkie-talkie twice and heard Veronica's two bursts of static in response. She recognized the animal, too.

The *cuadrillos* appeared at intervals around the perimeter of the ring, keeping the monster running and then ducking behind the barriers to escape his charges. After a few minutes, the white monster stopped and moved towards the middle of the ring, pawing the earth angrily and snorting spray.

Antonio entered the ring at a proud trot, his magenta cape on his arm and two red-flowered *banderillas* held aloft. The crowd cheered as he ran towards the bull and stopped twenty paces away.

The bull eyed him grimly.

Hanns got a shot from behind the bull adjusting the depth of field to switch focus from Antonio's face to the sunlight glinting off the much closer horns of the beast.

Antonio provoked a charge with a wave of the cloth and let the bull pass him three times. Antonio moved with surprising grace. Hanns was impressed. The bull paused, and Hanns swung his camera momentarily towards Vanessa who hunched forward in her chair, biting her lip.

The bull charged again. With the two *banderillas* held high, Antonio plunged the barbs into the hump on the neck of the speeding leviathan. The bull shook his horns with rage, trying to shake off the stinging darts as a stream of crimson blood stained the white of his side.

Antonio took another pair of *banderillas* from the hands of one of the *cuadrillos* at the edge of the ring and quickly darted the bull again in a single pass. Hanns heard the bull breathing like a steam locomotive from the edge of the ring. "How you doin' Veronica? Holding up okay?"

The radio hissed. "I'm doing better than I thought I would. I'm thinking about the shots more than about what I'm shooting."

"Don't talk like that. I'll fall in love with you," said Hanns. "Keep it up."

The bull charged again. Antonio let him pass under the *muleta*, watching for any tendency to hook to one side or the other. On the next charge, he planted the last pair of *banderillas* deftly and precisely.

Hanns swung his lens towards a group of old Spanish men who clapped and nodded their enthusiastic approval. "Antonio will want to see that. There's nothing so gratifying as impressing the true *aficionados*."

The bull stopped. Antonio faced him and bowed respectfully. He did not like to see *matador*s tease a bull to entertain the crowd. The people in the stands applauded the gesture. This was an unusual and beautiful bull, and Hanns appreciated that Antonio could treat the animal with some reverence—even if he was about to kill it.

Antonio stood erect and invited the bull to pass again and again. Each time, the horns barely brushed past him. A piece of gold brocade flew from a leg of his pants. Waving the *muleta*, he forced the bull into a series of tight turns, moving deliberately so the blood streaked animal appeared to spin around him. He leaped, bent, spun, and twisted like a dancer—each time frustrating the bull who could not figure out why his prey kept disappearing. The bull stopped to catch his breath, faced Antonio again, and shook his horns, pawing the ground with steaming nostrils flared.

Antonio reached for the sword and stood erect and in profile in front of the bull, holding the *estoque* on an unwavering outstretched arm and looking over his shoulder across the sword's tip into the bull's eyes.

"I am sorry, *amigo*. I am sorry," he whispered. For the tiniest fraction of a moment, he looked down.

The crowd in the stands erupted into blurred streaks of color and white, slowly spinning. The *estoque* floated across his field of view, suspended in space but his hand would not respond to his will to reach for it. A dull pain welled up in his stomach. *I think it is in my stomach but I am not sure.* A strange reverberant sigh reached his ears. He struck something…tasted sand, and felt a gritty sensation on his cheek. Shouting echoed around him and the most unusual vision of sideways feet danced next to his face. Someone called his name. Warm sand embraced his body and then all went electric white.

"I almost fell into the trap of becoming one of those assholes who visits you in the hospital and tells you how lucky you are," said Hanns.

Antonio smiled.

"How is the *matador?*"

Antonio grabbed a control box and raised the back of his hospital bed slowly. "Maybe luck is not the right word, but it could have been a lot worse. The horn went in between my legs, missed my *cajónes*, missed my femoral artery and did not do any internal damage. They opened me up to check, and I'll be sore for a while, but there's no nerve damage. I'll walk, run, make children maybe. I have to lie here for another week and then…"

"And then *what?*" asked Veronica. "I really hope you aren't going to do this again."

"I don't know," offered Hanns. "The man has a talent. Did you see how the crowd…"

"Veronica, we know Hanns well enough to see he is only torturing you, so do not fall for his games. I have no idea what *what* will be, but at the moment, I am feeling like I faced my bull and I faced him well.

Something about the blood on the pure white coat struck me differently this time. I apologized to the bull, and in the moment of my hesitation, it was like my teacher warned me. The bull saw a chance to save his life. I don't blame him for that.'

'As I have always said, the end of the *corrida* is only the end. *Mi sueño*—my dream was never to kill the bull. Yesterday, I danced in the sand with a strong, fast and beautiful partner in front of an arena full of people. It was dangerous and exciting…as I wanted it to be. I could feel my partner and predict how to move, how to stay close and just barely out of danger's reach. I felt the *duende*, and I have gotten what I wanted. I may feel differently another day, but I have gone to the edge and returned.'

'My only regret is the story is over. Tino has found a guitar, but the *documentario* is ruined. At least we shot some good footage, and I'm looking forward to seeing the photos. If it had all ended with the return of Tino's painting back in Germany, it would have still been *increíble*. I am very proud to have all of you as friends, and to have had this experience."

"As you said," replied Tino, "it's not about the ending. It's about the whole story—which I suspect is far from over. I prefer to think of this as the end of a chapter."

"Absolutely," said Hanns. "I have no regrets about the unfinished film. I had the time of my life. The whole thing was a great movie for me. The only reason I came to begin with was for the dance, and I have no complaints about any of it. I don't care if I killed my bull or not. Life is not a single *corrida*. My only real problem is figuring out what to do next. *This* will be a hard act to follow." Hanns paused and grabbed his chin between his thumb and forefinger. "But my suspicion is that *next* is not something you figure out so much as open yourself to. I am connected to extraordinary people and extraordinary places. My life happens at the confluence of extraordinary rivers. Sometimes, trying to find answers is like trying to fall asleep. You can curse at the ceiling tiles all night but sleep won't come until you surrender and let it gently take you.

I'll surprise you all, perhaps, with a prediction based on nothing but unsupportable faith. Clear your minds. *Next* will find us all and carry us to places even more beautiful, remarkable and profound."

"I agree," smiled Veronica, "and I'll let you slide on the faith thing."

Hanns smiled. "And one last thing, Antonio…'

'Here…Keep the sunglasses."

EPILOGUE

Dear Hanns,

It is difficult to believe a year has passed since our grand adventure in Spain. For Anna and me, the memories of that time are vivid and your wonderful photographs make them even more so.

I have to relate to you some experiences I've had recently that are tied to our story.

One of the loose threads we never attended to during our trip to Spain was the matter of talking to Antonio's cousin about representing my paintings and your photographs. It was good Antonio was able to store the artworks for us when we left.

I called Antonio to see how he was recovering, and he told me his cousin Jose the art dealer had seen our work, was very excited about the whole story of the Last Supper, and about organizing an exhibition in his gallery for both of us.

A month ago, I flew back to Sevilla to attend the art opening and brought with me de la Luz's negra guitar. In many ways, it was like traveling back in time to my college art show - the one where The Last Supper caused so much controversy. Jose actually insisted I display The Last Supper even if I had no intention of selling it. He's not overly traditional and seems attracted to controversy - you'd like him very much.

There was also an entire gallery room featuring prints we had made from your negatives. I wish you could have been there. They were well-received and I have a wad of money to wire you as soon as I know where to send it. Your enlargements are all over Sevilla now, and I have some of your prints on my own wall at home that I admire daily.

But let me tell you about the exhibition. As with my original show, I was not sure what to expect so I sat in a corner and played the guitar. A few people didn't like the work. That's expected, but maybe the world is changing? Nobody really seemed all that upset by it. A lot of people openly loved it. It was very gratifying to see, but I wanted to keep my anonymity and quietly watch the people view my art before having to shake a thousand hands and chit-chat with all the "art sophisticates."

A weathered looking man approached me. He was very interested in the negra I was playing and in The Last Supper.

He disappeared and returned later in the evening, almost at the end of the show, and asked if I remembered him. He had been the man who originally exchanged a guitar for my Last Supper painting so many years ago, and he introduced himself as Juan Romero.

I was quite surprised, of course, and met him the next morning to tell him the story of how the painting had come back to me.

It turns out he had been involved with championing the rights of women and workers in the late 50's and early 60's, and had been vocal about questioning some of the Catholic Church's spiritual authority. The Franco Government frowned on these kinds of activities and arrested him at a rally. He had assumed the guardia raided his home, and that the painting had been seized and destroyed.

After ten years, Romero escaped

from prison. He had been cooperative for years while waiting for his chance to get away, so the guards trusted him. He was out on a work detail one day in Sevilla, and when they weren't watching, he slipped into the Guadalquivir river and swam off. He stayed in the water under a dock until nightfall and finally came out in the middle of a gypsy camp in an abandoned freight yard. Sound familiar?

He stayed with the gypsies for a few months and then went home when he thought the authorities would no longer be looking for him there. All he found was an old neighbor who told him that whether by mistake or through cruelty, his family had received a notice that he had passed away in prison. They had packed up and moved away five years before. This explains why The Last Supper ended up in an estate sale. The family had limited means to move a lot of possessions and sold everything cheap to Antonio's cousin. Romero had no place to go and returned to the gypsies who took him in.

I hadn't mentioned anything about the

loss of the guitar he originally gave me. I felt bad about no longer having it, and he hadn't asked about it up to that point, but he did recognize my negra instantly as something unusual. He identified the African Blackwood immediately. He looked over the instrument very carefully and even put a small inspection mirror inside it. Finally, after a very long hesitation, he bit his lip and asked who had built it. When I told him, he began to weep.

It turns out Juan Romero was actually the lost father of de la Luz in Ronda. The gypsies let him stay with them because he provided them with fine guitars they would not normally be able to either find or afford. This explains why we heard the voice of my original guitarra that night I played in the gypsy camp.

The older de la Luz told me about Bernard and how the gypsies had taken in the American because he was so passionate about flamenco. Maybe they sympathized with him because he was resisting authority? Certainly he was not the first foreigner to fall in love with the music and dance, or romanticize the gypsy lifestyle. De la Luz told me of a night about a year ago when Bernard brought three foreigners to the camp. De la Luz didn't want to take chances so he listened to the music in hiding and wondered who the player was. Of course, that player was me, but apparently, the gypsies thought Bernard was getting too familiar. Someone must have poked him about inviting too many strangers home and risking de la Luz's cover, so he made up the whole story about a guitar maker in Ronda as a smoke screen. That whole trip should have been a dead end.

Three days later – the day of the evening I went back to the camp and found it empty – the gypsies folded up the river camp and left. De la Luz found out the next day they had drugged Bernard and abandoned him there, and he realized then that outsiders don't really become insiders with the gypsies. He loved their passionate music and was grateful for the shelter they had given him, but after a year-and-a-half, he knew it was time to move on. He thanked them and went back to ensure nothing bad happened to Bernard.

De la Luz got him cleaned up, and Bernard is now staying with other non-gypsy friends from the flamenco community in Triana. I was glad to hear he's doing okay.

From there, de la Luz settled in to a quiet job in back of a furniture workshop under his Romero alias. Apparently, about ten thousand people named Juan Romero live in Sevilla. Nobody in authority would want to sort through paper files to verify the identity of any particular one of a few hundred Juan Romeros listed as non-violent fugitives— and there was no reason for anyone to report an old carpenter as suspicious in the first place. He blended in working in Sevilla for another year before he ran across a poster for my exhibition on the street.

You should have seen his face when I told him my side of the story. I still can't believe he was actually there with us that night in Triana. So close! Of course, he was very excited to find out his son and his wife were in Ronda, and he was very proud of his son's guitar-making.

I had planned to drive to Ronda the next day anyway to visit de la Luz Junior, so naturally, I invited the old man. You should have seen the look on Ernesto de la Luz's face when I showed up unannounced in his shop after a year's absence, and then his father walked in behind me alive and well. It was a beautiful thing to witness. Anna was beside herself.

After the reunion, we played duets in the shop for hours with my negra and the old man's blanca – the one you tried to buy for me when we were first in the shop I offered to return The Last Supper to him as a gift and he offered me the blanca I once wanted so much.

I couldn't take it from him. The negra continues to open up beautifully as its maker predicted it would, and it has become my new voice. The elder de la Luz is an inspiring player, and we are now performing as a duo. The two instruments blend beautifully and I still get to enjoy the magic voice of the blanca when he plays it. It's surprising how you can desire something so passionately until it floats into your lap. It made me realize how musically happy I am these days now that I get to play on a magical instrument again in places where flamenco is appreciated.

The elder de la Luz is now working in Ronda, ironically as "Romero the apprentice" - a status that earns him some good-natured teasing, but Guitarras de la Luz are establishing a reputation and there is now over a year's waiting list to have one built. The front counter of the shop has been moved back to accommodate the many people who come in to play. Sometimes, I even set up my easel and paint in the workshop while the other flamencos "summon up their duende." I have music to play and dancers in sexy dresses to chase. Ronda is heaven.

Anna (who sends her best) has also fallen in love with the ancient magic of Ronda and with the patronage of the Spanish art community, we have purchased a very old and beautiful place here right at the edge of El Tajo with a wonderful terrace that hangs out into space.

Anna has just opened a Ronda branch of her "Magic Accessories" shop close to de la Luz's place and it's a huge success. Word is getting out. She's also creating traditional Spanish dancing dresses with a sexy twist, and you should hear her picking up Spanish almost as fast as Andreas, who is learning to play now, too. I've ordered him a small guitar, and the de la Luz's are fighting over who gets to build it for him. He's seven now and gets glowing looks of approval from the aficionados when he claps perfect compas behind the dancers.

Kalimba now has a regular contract flying freight between Sevilla and Germany a few times a month and that's made it easy to get back and forth without spending a great deal of money. We enjoy our visits with him and he comes to many of my concerts. He's developed a taste for flamenco, and a taste for Anna as well.

Kalimba's a great conversationalist and has become quite an appreciator of art. He's like you in many ways, and we enjoy having him around as much for his company as for the stares he brings with his wild-man appearance and powerful witch-doctor demeanor. He's brought African bush medicine to the chocolate shop and Anna is producing chocolates that probably wouldn't even be legal if the authorities had such obscure plants on their black-lists of controlled substances.

By the way, Kalimba's new business is taking off (pardon the pun). He seems very happy.

Antonio has healed wonderfully; he's a changed man. He's as religious as ever with his Virgins and Saints, but since the bullfight, he acts more like church happens on Sunday morning so life can happen on Saturday night without too long a wait for forgiveness. I can't get the whole guilt-culture thing, but Anna thinks he's a lot happier now that he's "out on the dance floor." We joined him for an evening in Sevilla a few weeks ago and had to laugh at Vanessa fending off the other women, trying to keep him to herself. Maybe it's the sunglasses?

It's funny how things change and how

they stay the same. Antonio still goes to the corrida once in a while, but he's lost interest in participating. Just as well for him, I think.

Anyway, my friend, I hope this gets to you soon, and I wish you safe travels. Send some photographs when you get the chance.

Love and duende,

Tino

Dear Hanns,

Greetings from Veronica - Antonio's sister. I've thought quite a bit about our bedroom conversation - the one about God and atheism. When my brother almost died, I felt helpless and alone, but I couldn't find it in myself to reach out to a traditional God.

Ultimately, I found solace in the idea that I could have God (or whatever) on my own terms - not necessarily as a deity or even as an intelligent force or as anything in particular that needed a name.

As an atheist, I disconnected myself spiritually because I didn't like the labeling and the rule books. But I think you're right that the "atheist" label is just as limiting if not more so. I'm okay with the idea that there may be power within me or flowing through me or shared collectively between living things. I have no idea if or how it works, but I'm happy with not knowing and I'm enjoying the mystery as you suggested. Even if it's all wishful thinking and self-deception, it offers real comfort and a feeling of being connected to something magical. It's true what they say; "Ignorance is bliss."

I've been studying some Spanish history and ran across something you will find interesting.

The traditional story taught in Spanish schools is that the Moors came from North Africa as conquerors, forcing the Islamic faith on Southern Spain until the Christian inquisition took the country back. But there is actually no record of violent Arab conquest. The Arabs came during the dark ages and prospered because they brought the science and philosophy of the ancient Greeks to a primitive land. The Moors were mathematicians, scientists and architects. They had written language. They saw astronomy as the scientific key to calculating where Mecca was so they could pray in the right direction. They studied anatomy, developed advanced medical and surgical capability and built sanitary sewage systems. Most of the large cathedrals in Spain are built on top of ancient mosques and the Moorish architecture and script is still plainly visible. It was the Christians who saw scientific inquiry as threatening to their mythology and who forcibly converted Moslems or burned them as heretics.

What I find fascinating is when the Christians started to take over, the Spanish Moors had been out of the African desert for many centuries. When they called to Africa for help, their Arab brothers came to assist but were appalled by the music, art and culture of the Moors' comparatively open Islamic society. Many of the statues smashed in the mosques were not destroyed by Christians, but by North African rescuers who saw the easy Moorish lifestyle as contrary to the teachings of Islam.

The bible says "God created man in his own image." After thinking about the restrictions of too much labelled belief, I was beginning to feel that was backwards – Maybe we make God in our own image?

Here's another perspective:

The African desert is hot and dry with sandstorms and endless stretches of waterless desert. If you don't live by a strict code, you perish very quickly.

Spain has rivers. Things grow easily. It rains. The climate is moderate and simple survival is not nearly as big a problem.

Could it be that the God of the Spanish Moslems was a kinder, more tolerant, and gentler God than the harsh and demanding God of the African Moslems because his followers made Him in the image of the world they lived in? Know the artist by his work.

I don't know the answer, but it makes me wonder if that isn't part of why people like myself who have grown up with air-conditioning, electric lights, clean water, refrigerated food and antibiotics find it so easy to see God as irrelevant or nonexistent. Our insulated environment offers little of either adversity or natural bounty to shape our spirituality and therefore, we don't have much of an image to make God in. Being religious is not my nature, but I think there is much to be spiritual about if you look out the window.

Prophets and other religious celebrities aren't my thing, but Jesus said "seek the truth and you shall find it." Avoiding the truth may be more of a Church thing than a Jesus thing.

He also said "judge not lest you be judged," and I can work with that. Antonio is finding his way and I'll find mine. We all will, I suppose - which makes all the questioning and answering and retreating into safe little philosophical corners just part of the great human dance. I think your friend Anna would like that. But if there is a "God-in-heaven" kind of God out there, I have to wonder if that whole crazy dance isn't just what he wants us to be learning - one step at a time? It's either that or blind faith, and blind faith doesn't seem to jibe with seeking the truth.

Ultimately, I like the encouragement to "seek the truth." It's just the suggestion that truth can ultimately be "found" that sounds idealistic to me, though I guess it's hard to fault a prophet with being idealistic.

We'll never know for sure, but I can personally enjoy the not-knowing. It feels closer to truth than I've ever been.

Thanks, Hanns, for the friendship and challenging ideas. I hope we'll meet again. I wish you great adventure and inexplicable mystery.

Warmly,

Veronica.

Hanns,

I was sitting in an outdoor cafe in Ronda with Ernesto late yesterday afternoon when some hikers came in for a drink. We get groups of hikers and rock-climbers who explore El Tajo and to my amazement, one of them came back carrying your hammer – not that anything really amazes me any more. I had my guitar with me so I played for him and his friends. They must have thought I was crazy when the only tip I would accept was an old hammer!

It's not in the greatest of condition, but it's served some noble purposes and I'm happy to return it to you. It was the only magic in our whole crazy story that hadn't come full-circle yet.

Maybe it is just an old hammer, but I couldn't resist using it to put one more nail into a special dance floor.

All the best,

Tino.

Hanns,

I am glad to hear you and Sorcery are having great adventures. I miss her and may beg for a few weeks in the crew's quarters one of these days.

I took some savings and the money you gave me for Sorcery, bought a few gliders and a small tow-plane, and opened a sail-plane school on the Costa del Sol. Especially during the hot Spanish summers, the thermals are great and I took Anna up for a four-hour float a few weeks ago. Let me know when you'd like to try it. It's the rush of flying with the quiet of sailing. I'm addicted.

I see Anna and Tino regularly and they've become great friends. I've even seen Antonio a time or two.

If you're planning any more wild adventures and need a pilot, you know who to call. I may just round up the whole crew one of these days and fly the whole flamenco family out to meet you in some clear blue anchorage.

Wind in your sails,

Kalimba

Dear Hanns,

I am no write so good, but I am wanting to thank you for many things.

I am sorry we were no able to make our film but I learn many things on our adventure that change my life. I got to have my big corrida and face my bull. Not so many people do that in their lifes. It is not about winning or losing or killing the bull. It is a dance and I have done this dance now. I am happy.

I paid for the white bull to go back and live with the indultos — the pardoned bulls — on Miura's ranch. It was expensive, but I could not let him be slaughtered after he faced me and we did not kill each other. Senor Miura tells me he is happy in the fields there.

I hope you do not mind, but I am taking some classes in film and photography and using the cameras you left. I still have the "FLAMENCO TOREO" sign on my truck and Veronica is helping me to research and film some of the colorful story of my country. So much history is buried under our feet, and my teachers are pleased with my projects. I will maybe open a small studio with my sister when I am finished with my classes.

Tino is often in town and I see him and Anna and Kalimba from time to time.

You will laugh when I tell you I am in a very wonderful and difficult romance with Vanessa, but I feel our toreo expedition had something to do with it that I cannot explain. When we are not wanting to kill each other, we are very happy together. Thank you.

Let me know next time you are in Sevilla. I would love to show you my films and photographs.

Muchas Gracias, amigo

Antonio

DEAR TINO AND ANNA,

I'M WRITING FROM THE GREEK ISLANDS.

MY MOTHER FORWARDED YOUR MAIL TO ME HERE WHERE ALL IS ANCIENT HISTORY AND PROFOUND BEAUTY. IT WAS WONDERFUL TO HEAR HOW OUR SPANISH ADVENTURE FINALLY CAME AROUND AND I LAUGHED WHEN I SAW MY GRANDFATHER'S OLD HAMMER AGAIN. I'LL SEND PHOTOGRAPHS NEXT TIME I'M AT A PLACE WHERE I CAN GET FILM DEVELOPED AS I DON'T TRUST THE ISLAND CAMERA SHOPS TO DO THE JOB PROPERLY.

I'LL KEEP THIS SHORT AS I'M LEAVING TOMORROW MORNING FOR SOME REMOTE ISLANDS WHERE I WON'T BE ABLE TO SEND MAIL, AND I WANT TO GET THIS LETTER TO YOU BEFORE THE LOCAL POST OFFICE SHUTS DOWN FOR THE DAY. IF YOU CAN SHARE THIS LETTER WITH ANTONIO, VERONICA AND KALIMBA, IT WILL SAVE ME FROM HAVING TO WRITE THREE LETTERS IN THE SHORT TIME I HAVE TO FINISH ONE. MORE NEWS TO COME IN A FEW WEEKS.

THE RETURN OF THE HAMMER REMINDS ME OF THE CONVERSATION I HAD WITH YOU, TINO,

WHILE WE DROVE THROUGH THE OLIVE GROVES NEAR RONDA. WE TALKED ABOUT THE POWERS OF THE UNCONSCIOUS MIND AND THE PSYCHOLOGY OF SACRIFICE AND PRAYER.

I'M REDISCOVERING ANOTHER WAY TO TOUCH THE HIDDEN CONSCIOUSNESS. ARCHETYPES — SIMPLE SYMBOLS — ARE COMMON TO ALL PEOPLE AND MANY ARE AT LEAST COMMON TO MEMBERS OF A SOCIETY. THEY ARE EASY TO DISCOVER THROUGH DREAM SYMBOLISM. IF YOU DREAM ABOUT YOUR ROOM OR YOUR HOUSE, THAT'S USUALLY A METAPHOR FOR YOUR SELF. YOUR CAR, FOR EXAMPLE, MAY BE SYMBOLIC OF YOUR PERSONAL STYLE — YOUR WAY OF GETTING AROUND IN THE WORLD. ALL SORTS OF MEANINGS ARE ASSOCIATED WITH VARIOUS SYMBOLS AND DEPENDING ON WHO COMPILED THE LISTS OF THESE AND HOW, THEY RANGE FROM DEAD ACCURATE TO COMPLETE BULLSHIT, BUT WATER IS AN ACCEPTED UNIVERSAL ARCHETYPE FOR CONSCIOUSNESS ITSELF.

I GOT A LETTER FROM VERONICA THAT MADE ME WONDER IF THIS ARCHETYPE PHENOMENON DOESN'T WORK IN TWO DIRECTIONS. I'M HERE IN WATERS THAT ARE CRYSTAL CLEAR AND SOOTHING BLUE. I CAN OFTEN SEE THE BOTTOM. I'M ON

THE WATER AND IN THE WATER EVERY DAY.
I GET MY FOOD FROM IT. THE COLORS HERE
ARE VIBRANT. I CAN ONLY GUESS THAT PART
OF THE PROFOUND CONTENTMENT I FEEL HERE
IS A REFLECTION WITHIN ME OF THE PROFOUND
BEAUTY THAT SURROUNDS ME.

IF MY SUBCONSCIOUS RELATIONSHIP WITH
GOD IS BASED ON THE SYMBOLIC CONTENT AND
THE RELATIVE HARSHNESS OR COMFORT OF MY
ENVIRONMENT, THEN I AM BLESSED TO BE IN
THIS PLACE.

I'LL SPEND A FEW MORE MONTHS HERE
AND THEN CROSS TO THE CARIBBEAN BEFORE
THE ATLANTIC HURRICANE SEASON STARTS.
I'LL CHECK IN AT THE COSTA DEL SOL FOR
A FEW DAYS BEFORE I HEAD OUT INTO THE
ATLANTIC, AND HOPEFULLY HAVE A CHANCE TO
VISIT WITH YOU ALL IF I DON'T SEE YOU HERE IN
THE GREEK ISLANDS FIRST.

I LOOK FORWARD TO HEARING HOW THE
NEGRA HAS OPENED UP, AND TELL ANTONIO
I'LL BE EXCITED TO SEE HIS FILM WORK.
I'LL BE OFF SAILING FOR AT LEAST A FEW YEARS,
SO THE CAMERA EQUIPMENT IS MY GIFT TO
HIM. I'M HAPPY IT WILL GET USED INSTEAD OF

SITTING IN STORAGE.

GIVE MY CONGRATULATIONS TO ERNESTO ON FINDING HIS FATHER AGAIN.

LOVE AND LIGHT,

HANNS

My Dear Hanns,

It's hard to believe it's been only a year since we had strawberry milkshakes and made love back in the Palatinate forest. It feels long ago and far away. So much has changed since then.

I have little to say that wouldn't dilute what doesn't need to be spoken. We all came together, touched each other and have since scattered. Each of us in what Tino calls our "flamenco family" brought a certain unique chemistry to the mix but you were the catalyst that triggered the explosion.

Beyond simple gratitude, I wish to convey my profound feeling that we are still connected in some mysterious way. I love my husband and family, my new life in Ronda and my growing friendship with Kalimba, but at whatever distance,

I know I will always be dancing with you.

I've enclosed a tin of chocolates. Each is labelled after a type of dance and has magical - or if you prefer, mysterious - herbs and spices that evoke an essence of tango, swing, ballet, salsa and other styles.

Three are labelled "flamenco." It might be through African bush magic or I may just be manipulating your subconscious mind, but it doesn't really matter. Wait until you feel the time is right and pop one of them into your mouth. Chew slowly and enjoy. I'll be there dancing in your dreams.

Love,

Anna

Chop wood, carry water.

After enlightenment, dance, chop wood, carry water

-adapted from Zen Proverb

AUTHOR'S NOTE

As with most works of fiction, a spine of truth runs through my story.

In 1987, I was 23 years old and had just purchased my first sailboat—a 26 foot sloop. I moved aboard and lived at anchor in Miami, finishing college, working, and dreaming about cruising thanks to inspiration from my floating neighbors, the majority of whom were twenty years older than me.

The stories of Miami's remarkable floating community along with those of my own adventures would (and will) fill many books, but it is one of the great friendships sprung from these experiences that provided the bones for *The Dance*.

Writing about people other than yourself is far safer than recounting your own experiences directly. Autobiography provokes concerns about overstating your own role or perhaps revealing that things and people you find fascinating or inspiring are less so to others. Nobody likes people who talk about themselves, less so people who take up an entire volume to do so.

The writer, by his very nature, aspires to share his perspective and vision, but the writer of fiction can, if he is an effective story-teller, create characters that may not be overtly perceived by his reader to be direct extensions of himself. Marching beneath the banner of fiction, the writer has license to invent, exaggerate and twist a story that may be more or less rooted in fact.

Ari, the friend who inspired this work, was a Swiss mechanical engineer anchored nearby me on a fiberglass yacht of 1960's vintage that he had thoroughly customized inside and out in his own precise, sturdy, brilliant and beautiful style. We became acquaintances and ultimately close friends. Regrettably, I never had the opportunity to sail with Ari, but I had occasion to stay on-board with him several times in Trinidad while his vessel was in dry-dock. Recognizing him to be a masterful storyteller with a history and talent for getting in and out of the most astonishing trouble, I put many hours of his stories on videotape and resolved to one day…well…*do something* with them.

Having plenty of my own stories to do *something* with, the additional burden of having appointed myself official archivist for another's was a mixed blessing, though it ultimately served the purpose of having gotten me started with the *doing* of the *something* and later in the story—the greater story beyond this book—my own story did and so will collide with his, making *The Dance* ultimately a vehicle for my own exploits.

This particular volume is based on one of Ari's less epic stories—a short tale told to me almost as an aside. Something about the juxtaposed pilgrimages to film a bullfighting documentary and find a magical guitar in Spain fascinated me. I first conceived *The Dance* as a fairly direct retelling of Ari's short story, but having been handed a skeleton to festoon with literary meat, I found my characters developing lives and perspectives of their own sufficient to inspire a larger work.

The seed for *The Dance*, then, is one of Ari's tales; well-told but told mostly, nonetheless, about people I never met, events I never witnessed and places I have never been. Telling another's story offers a degree of comfortable anonymity as mentioned earlier, but holds the writer to a higher standard of authenticity. Potentially, *The Dance* will be read by people much more familiar with the times and settings than myself. I was six years old when the actual events transpired in 1970, and confess to have never attended a bull fight.

Google Earth allowed me to fly over places like *Sevilla*, land on a photographic grid of labelled streets and view my surroundings interactively and panoramically.

It's no true substitute for physically being anywhere, but has hopefully allowed me to be true to some of the smaller details.

I chose *l'Estartit* as a stopover point based on a Google Earth survey of the *Costa del Sol* and its suggested route from *Kaiserslautern* to *Sevilla*. It lay at an appropriate location to divide up a long road trip, and looked like an excellent place to keep a yacht. I found numerous pictures on the internet of *l'Estartit* taken in the late 1960's and early 1970's before the modern marina was built and the waterfront became crowded with hotels, and I took care to describe the old seawall and beacon as they were at the time.

I offer apologies for any glaring inaccuracies and can plead only ignorance or creative license, leaving my reader to preside over my sentencing hopefully in good consideration of my story's other virtues.

There is the old saw about "not letting the truth stand in the way of a good story." I have taken broad liberties with the story I was given. I see no merit in delineating what is fact from fiction in the finished book, except in a few instances. Regarding Pfaff sewing machines, my knowledge of them is limited only to hearing they are a brand of good quality. Pfaff machines would have been appropriate tools for Anna to have in a dress shop in 1970, but inferences made about the quality of their parts or availability of their service were entirely fabricated by myself for storytelling purposes.

I'll keep my honoraria brief.

I thank my wife Suzanne who, apart from being a dear friend is a tough critic. I divide my energy among many interests besides family and yet, she encouraged me to spend time on this book, and provided substantive input that helped motivate me to keep typing.

At the time of this writing, my daughter is four years old, but I am thankful to have someone to leave something behind for. When you are ready, *The Dance* is for you.

Richard Geller, Silvia Sayas and a few other early manuscript reviewers have been valuable and supportive. Thanks for wading through my stacks of loose paper.

Of course, there is Ari who gave me the story expanded upon here. It is an honor to be entrusted with it and to have been granted your indulgence to shape it as I may. I hope you find it as entertaining to read in its embellished form as it was in actual experience.

The business of writing books is one entirely separate from the business of marketing them and selling them. I am fortunate to live in a time when technology provides me with power to research, write, edit and share with unprecedented ease. Gone are the days when typewritten manuscripts were covered with red ink and then retyped *ad nauseum* until they were approved for final typesetting—and good riddance to them, I say. I am a product of my time, and the idea of making and sharing books through traditional means strikes me as impossibly cumbersome. I am immensely privileged to write at a time when *The Dance* can be drafted, typeset and shared without the massive costs and obstacles of not so long ago.

Any writer hopes his story will be thought good enough to take flight, and the fantasy of being able to receive some level of remuneration for putting pen to paper is one shared by many artists.

There is no publishing company apart from my own tiny, corporate shell. There is only me—the writer—living in a world where technology empowers the individual to share his creative work. As the ultimate enabler of that process, it is my reader to whom, above all, this book is most humbly dedicated.

I would beg of my reader one final indulgence. Though books retain their traditional form, they are distributed in new ways. In the manner of dropping a rock in Tino's rhetorical pond, I would be grateful for your honest review posted in the public forum or electronic book store of your choice. Such authentic discourse only empowers writers and readers alike, and reinforces the power to publish so recently delivered to the common man.

There is still the matter alluded to earlier about my own personal stories, and though I am grateful for such adventures as have transpired in my past, at 45 years of age, I do not primarily see life as something to be looked back upon. As Robert Frost said, "miles to go before I sleep." For all of us, I pray for opportunities to experience and explore still more of what life offers before we take our final bows and step off to the wings.

Ultimately, life is but a chain of interconnected experiences. We are all writers of our own destinies. If the adventures documented herein inspire others to accept and embrace the power and responsibility of this authorship, take a few risks, accept a few challenges, roll with a few punches, play a few arpeggios, teach a few lessons, laugh at God's jokes and dance under the stars to the rhythm of celestial castanets, I will have accomplished a most noble purpose.

It has been my pleasure to dance for you.

ABOUT THE AUTHOR

Dave Bricker lives in Miami, Florida with his wife and daughter. He teaches graphic and interactive design at an Arts University and is an avid acoustic guitarist.

Dave Bricker is the author of *The One Hour Guide to Self-Publishing: Straight Talk for Fiction and Nonfiction Writers About Producing and Marketing Your Own Books.*

The Dance is his first work of fiction. His second novel, *Waves,* continues the adventures of Hanns as he sails from Florida to the Caribbean.

For more information, please visit:

http://www.theDanceNovel.com
http://www.WavesNovel.com
http://www.oneHourSelfPub.com
http://www.EssentialAbsurdities.com

COLOPHON

This book was set in Adobe Garamond, a typeface designed by Robert Slimbach, and based loosely on the original designed by Claude Garamond in the 1540's. Though digital type designers have taken many liberties with Garamond's original design, the longer ascenders and descenders and slightly smaller counters add a friendly, romantic feel to the type without sacrificing legibility.

The ornament featured throughout the book is based on the silhouettes of fighting bulls seen throughout the countryside in Southern Spain.

The book's title and chapter headers are set in Trajan, a typeface designed for Adobe in 1989 by Carol Twombly based on the Roman square capitals engraved on the base of Trajan's column.